Praise for the Safe Harbor Medical Mysteries

The Case of the Questionable Quadruplet

"Love the mystery and medical setting interwoven to tell a great story. Lots of twists and turns and plenty of suspects to point fingers at each other. The end is unexpected and the reveal compelling. I will definitely read more by this author."
—Sandy Penny, SweetMysteryBooks.blogspot.com.

"This book keeps the reader on their toes as to who the culprit could possibly be from start to finish. The cast of characters is beautifully developed."
—Penelope Anne Bartotto, *Indtale*

The Case of the Surly Surrogate

"I liked this fantastic mystery. I never knew what was going to happen next and couldn't read fast enough to find out."
—Online Reviewer Jo-Anne B

"Attention cozy mystery readers: Jacqueline Diamond's second Safe Harbor Medical mystery only gets better! 5 Stars."
—Mary Castillo, bestselling author of *Lost in the Light*

The Case of the Desperate Doctor

"The mystery progresses at a swift speed and keeps you engaged with likable characters."
—Tracy Farnsworth, Round Table Reviews

More Books by Jacqueline Diamond

Mysteries and Suspense

AND THE BRIDE VANISHES
DANGER MUSIC
ECHOES
THE EYES OF A STRANGER
HIS SECRET SON
TOUCH ME IN THE DARK

Safe Harbor Medical Romances

THE WOULD=BE MOMMY
HIS HIRED BABY
THE HOLIDAY TRIPLETS
OFFICER DADDY
FALLING FOR THE NANNY
THE SURGEON'S SURPRISE TWINS
THE DETECTIVE'S ACCIDENTAL BABY
THE BABY DILEMMA
THE M.D.'S SECRET DAUGHTER
THE BABY JACKPOT
HIS BABY DREAM

The Case of the

QUESTIONABLE QUADRUPLET

Safe Harbor Medical Mysteries

Book One

Jacqueline Diamond

This is the first book of the Safe Harbor Medical mystery series. It shares a setting and some supporting characters with the author's Safe Harbor Medical romance series. More information about the books and the author is available at www.jacquelinediamond.net.

Published by K. Loren Wilson, Brea, California, USA

For subsidiary rights, please contact the author at jdiamondfriends@yahoo.com or at P.O. Box 1315, Brea, Calif. 92822.

ISBN-13: 978-1-936505-37-1

From the Author

When I told readers of my Safe Harbor Medical romances that I was spinning off a mystery series, several people asked if the books would include my trademarks: fast pacing, emotionally satisfying stories and touches of humor that unexpectedly make them laugh.

The answer to those questions is, yes! Plus a new hero—obstetrician Eric Darcy—and a supporting cast of quirky characters.

Although I'm best known for medical romances and romantic comedies, my one hundred previous novels—from St. Martin's Press, William Morrow, Harlequin and other publishers—include the mainstream mysteries *Danger Music* and *The Eyes of a Stranger.* I've also written Regency romances and romantic suspense.

For his invaluable feedback and advice, I want to thank Orange County Sheriff's Investigator Gary Bale (retired). I'm also grateful to my Beta readers, Deborah Golub R.N., Brooke Hamilton, Marcia Holman R.N. and Gail Ostheller, and my critique group, Orange County Fictionaires.

Welcome to the first Safe Harbor Medical Mystery!

Jacqueline Diamond
Brea, California

CHAPTER ONE

"Dr. Darcy, someone's breaking into your house!"

Telephone mouthpiece jiggling in front of her face, the young receptionist stared at me wide-eyed from behind my office counter. In the waiting room, visible through a small window, half a dozen women and a couple of men peered toward us.

My gut clenched at this threat. I couldn't afford to overreact, however. It was the middle of the afternoon, I had to compensate for morning surgeries that had run late, and my patients were depending on their obstetrician-gynecologist to focus on their needs. "Who's calling?"

"Your alarm company." Glenda's fingers fluttered. Always excitable, she was vibrating so hard her brown curls bounced.

Since I'd turned off my cell to avoid interruptions, the alarm company must have proceeded to my work number, which was second on their list. I picked up the handset, stated my password and name, Eric Darcy, and requested particulars.

A pane beside my front door had set off the alarm, a young man told me. I felt a surge of relief. That pane had been loose and might have fallen on its own. "Probably a false alarm," I told him. "Can you shut it off?"

"Certainly." Otherwise the alarm rings for ten minutes.

"Shouldn't we notify the police?" Glenda asked after I hung up. "I mean, what if it's terrorists or something?"

"I hardly think so," remarked my saintly nurse, Farrah Ortiz. "Don't worry, doctor. I'll contact Mr. Golden. Maybe he can check on it."

"Thank you," I mouthed, and continued down the hall toward Room 5, annoyed that I hadn't repaired the window and spared myself a shock.

My late wife's stepfather, Morris Golden, had offered to get it fixed, but his head is too stuffed with recipes to retain much else. A caterer, he'd occupied my downstairs bedroom since my wife Lydia's death nearly a year earlier.

Despite a few reservations, I'd invited him to stay with me. Never good with finances, Morris had been sleeping on a cot in his office, while I, as one of the world's worst cooks, appreciated that he prepared tasty meals with a comforting Jewish influence. Also, having him around eased the aching void.

On further consideration, the possibility of a break-in seemed remote. I'd lived in that house since childhood, and the worst crime I could recall on my street was dog poop left on the sidewalk.

Then I remembered what might have tempted a burglar.

Lydia's possessions, in the process of being sorted for storage or donation, were spread across the front room that once had served as her art studio. The idea of an intruder pawing through them revolted me.

Stop there.

During training, a doctor learns to ignore hunger, exhaustion and personal issues. They must wait their turn at the end of a long line of the sick and troubled. At that moment, the head of the line belonged to—I scanned the face sheet my nurse had dispensed—Malerie Nivens Abernathy.

Malerie was a legacy from my father's era, before Safe Harbor Medical Center had been remodeled from a community hospital to one of Southern California's top facilities for maternity and fertility care. She was the widowed mother of grown triplets, one of whom was also my patient.

She stuck out in my mind because of a family tragedy. I'd treated a second triplet prior to her murder six months earlier. Dee Marie Abernathy Tibbets had appeared initially to have died from a severe asthma attack. Then the autopsy revealed tiny hemorrhages in the eyes often associated with smothering or strangulation, as well as bruises on her arms consistent with a struggle. Ruled a homicide, the case remained unsolved.

Since then, I'd seen Malerie once, to adjust her blood pressure medication, since she requested that I supervise her routine care. Her reason for coming in today was listed as a consult. No details.

I knocked, opened the door and greeted the sixty-year-old woman seated on the examining table. Intensely red hair curled above a face creased from her former two-pack-a-day smoking habit. Rather than changing into an exam gown, she wore a pantsuit.

Malerie nodded coolly. "Hello, Eric."

I didn't remember her using my given name before. For a flicker of a second, even at thirty-five, I felt as if I were a kid and my late father was the real Dr. Darcy.

I flexed my shoulders beneath the white coat. "What brings you here today?" Since she hadn't changed clothes, she must not expect a physical exam and, according to Farrah's notes, her blood pressure was only slightly elevated. Her records displayed in the computer terminal indicated she'd recovered well from hip replacement surgery ten months earlier.

"I want to know what's going on, and spare me the crap."

Her voice had a hard edge.

In every practice, there are patients whose names you dread seeing on the schedule, people who are demanding, manipulative or quick to threaten a lawsuit. Aside from the occasional sharp tone, however, Malerie had never struck me as one of those.

My father advised once that, in the face of hostility, I should take it slow, pay attention and avoid acting arrogant. "Please tell me what's upset you."

"I trusted your father. And that other doctor." She must mean Isaiah Levin, Dad's partner, with whom I still practiced. "I can't believe they lied to me all these years."

What a strange remark. "About what?"

"I saw her." In her lap, Malerie's blue-veined hands formed fists. "Getting on a bus. Did you think you could keep her secret forever?"

"Keep who secret?"

Her gray-green eyes narrowed, deepening a fan of wrinkles. "Don't take me for a fool."

I leaned against the counter near the small sink. "To be honest, I'm baffled."

Malerie released a long breath. "Maybe they didn't tell you. In that case, I could use your help."

"Of course." I awaited enlightenment.

"My daughters weren't triplets," she said. "They were quadruplets."

I hid my astonishment as best I could. "Would you mind explaining?"

She lifted her chin as if bracing for an argument. "Since Dee Marie died, I've had vivid dreams about giving birth to four girls, not three. More like memories than dreams. I suppose you think I'm inventing this."

"You mentioned a bus," I said.

"Yesterday, driving on the boulevard, I saw her boarding a bus. She had the exact same color hair as my girls, and she moved gracefully, like Danielle, who took ballet for years. When she glanced up and flashed that lopsided smile, my heart nearly stopped."

"Did you talk to her?"

"There was a lot of traffic. Before I could turn my car around, the bus vanished."

If it looks like a duck and quacks like a duck… "Could it have been Danielle or Doreen?"

"She was thinner and she had short hair," Malerie said decisively. "Also, neither of my daughters rides the bus. And you know perfectly well I have no other children."

While it could be mistaken identity, the Abernathy triplets *were* distinctive. All had off-center, twist-of-the-lips smiles and hair of an unusual flame-red shade. Danielle and the late Dee Marie, who were identical—developed from a single egg—had thin noses. Doreen, the fraternal one, had slightly broader features.

The sighting might have been a delusion or a coincidence, or indicate a need for new glasses. I wasn't about to dismiss my patient's concerns, however. Malerie was mourning her dead daughter, and I understood from experience the insidious and unpredictable nature of grief.

It was also feasible that her perceptions had been influenced by buried memories. "Let's check your file." I shifted to a position at the terminal.

When our paper records from past decades had to be digitized, it was impractical to transfer everything. As a result, the computerized data included only basic information about Malerie's pregnancy and the triplets' birth. The pregnancy had occurred naturally, not as a result of fertility treatments. My father had delivered the girls by cesarean section.

Wait—here we went—there *had* been a fourth fetus, early in the pregnancy. "Did my father mention Vanishing Twin Syndrome?" I asked.

"I didn't have twins." Malerie waved off her own comment. "Never mind that. What is it?"

"Sometimes a fetus spontaneously aborts—miscarries or is reabsorbed—usually during the first trimester. It's estimated twenty to thirty percent of multiple conceptions lead to the loss of a fetus, for unknown reasons." I hoped that was enough specifics. It's a balancing act, providing information without overloading the patient.

Malerie shook her head. "That wasn't a fetus I saw getting on the bus. There must have been a fourth live birth."

I felt certain we could rule that out, but clearly *something* had happened. "Let's eliminate a few possibilities."

"Such as?"

"Have you suffered a recent blow to the head?"

She stiffened. "No. And I don't use drugs, except what you prescribe." That would be blood-pressure medication.

"Do you take it with alcohol?" If misused, BP meds can cause confusion.

"I'm not a heavy drinker, Eric." Her patience was thinning.

Many conditions can produce hallucinations, including tumors, dementia, mental illness and strokes. "Any blurred vision or numbness?"

"I am not imagining this!" she roared, loud enough to be heard outside the room. "I demand the truth, not a bunch of medical mumbo jumbo."

That was my cue to retreat. Not too far, though. "I promise to talk to Dr. Levin, since he was here at the time, in case he recalls anything. But I'd be happier if we could run some tests."

She launched herself from the table. I grabbed her arm to prevent a fall.

"Unless your father-in-law is putting magic mushrooms in my dinners, there's nothing to test," she snapped as she regained her balance.

Apparently Malerie subscribed to the meal service from Morris's company. Golden Fine Foods had carved a niche delivering specialty dinners, including vegan, gluten-free and hypoallergenic.

"I didn't realize you followed a special diet," I said, hoping to restore civility to the conversation.

"I just enjoy his cooking." She'd grown calmer. "I'll hear from you soon then?"

"Absolutely."

I escorted Malerie to the exit, partly as a courtesy and partly to run interference if she ran into Isaiah. I'd rather not have her accuse him of deception in front of other patients.

When she'd gone, Farrah reappeared. Late in the day, her honey-brown hair was creeping from its bun but her controlled manner never faltered. "Mr. Golden's at work. He wasn't able to get away, so I took the liberty of contacting your sister-in-law."

"Good. She has a key." It had been long enough since Lydia's death for me to start discarding her clothes and art supplies, but I couldn't. When her younger half-sister Tory offered to do it, I'd accepted.

"She was at the detective agency," Farrah reported. "She should be on her way to the house now."

"Excellent." A former policewoman who had worked crimes against properties, Tory was the ideal person for the task. Well, not entirely ideal. She didn't always respect boundaries, especially mine.

Farrah produced another face sheet. About to hurry to the next patient, I remembered my promise to Malerie. "Is Dr. Levin around?"

"He left early."

"Oh, that's right. It's Thursday." My partner took off early two days a week to play golf. I made a mental note to ask him about Malerie in the morning.

Between patients, Farrah updated me. It wasn't a false alarm. Tory had found the window smashed and summoned the cops.

Damn whoever had broken into my home! I loved that place, an imposing Tudor Revival striped with dark timbers and tall windows. No doubt the crook had assumed it was stuffed with valuables, but the electronics were old, except for my laptop, which I had carried to work. Aside from inherited pieces of silver cutlery and serving dishes, there were only Lydia's things laid out in the conservatory.

What idiot would break into a house posted as having an alarm system? Perhaps they had assumed it was a fake notice. Or they'd heard that a doctor lived there and stupidly believed there'd be drugs lying around.

How much damage had they done? I dreaded what I might find. Too bad Vivien, our part-time housekeeper, had moved to San Francisco a few weeks earlier to be near family. She'd be better able than Tory to assess what might be missing.

An hour later, my sister-in-law called to report. As always, I felt a jolt when she spoke, because her voice was so much like her sister's. "It was a quick in-and-out," she said. "It appears the perp only went through the studio."

"Can you tell what they took?"

"Yes, because I've been photographing Lydia's stuff." She took a long breath.

Even before she spoke again, I knew what was gone.

*

For my wife's thirtieth birthday, I had commissioned a necklace to connect the tangled threads of her identity. The interwoven chains of silver and gold represented the father,

Avram Silver, she'd lost to suicide when she was three, and the stepfather, Morris Golden, who'd helped raise her. The pendant was a large shimmering opal, her birthstone.

It had been her thirty-fifth birthday less than two weeks earlier that had prompted me to confront my loss by discarding some of her possessions and safeguarding others. I should have put the necklace in a safe-deposit box, along with a handful of other jewelry. Now, I discovered after reaching home, all that remained of them were the images on Tory's phone.

"I'm sorry." Disgust shadowed my sister-in-law's heart-shaped face. Through the bay window, waning sunlight picked out chestnut highlights in her frizzy brown hair. "I left it in full view. Tempting." Her gesture encompassed a rack of Lydia's many-hued garments, a drawing table, shelving units packed with art books, brushes and paints, blow-ups of web designs, and open boxes of personal items I couldn't bear to look at.

The room had been messy enough already. While I doubted the police had deliberately disturbed anything, someone had rummaged through the stuff. The disarray wasn't improved by the black fingerprint powder dusted across some surfaces. I'd seen more of that in the main hall, around the broken door pane.

"Any idea who might have done this?" I asked.

On our small residential street, we don't get much traffic, foot or motorized. Also, whoever broke in had been smart enough to gain access via the front door, gaining a sixty-second delay before the alarm blared.

"It's not a typical burglary," responded Tory, who'd escorted the police through the house. "The other rooms seem fine. Maybe the alarm scared the guy off."

"I wish it had scared him into a heart attack." That might be overkill, but it reflected my anger.

In bustled her roly-poly, balding father. His remaining puffs of gray hair quivered with outrage. "Are you all right, Eric?"

"Yes, thanks," I said. "I wasn't here when it happened."

"It could be traumatic." An exchange of glances flicked between him and Tory.

I wished they wouldn't fret about my supposedly fragile emotional state. Of course I grieved for the woman I'd loved for more than half my life, but I was in no danger of shattering. The less fuss, the better. I'd grown up here in silences, in the distances between people who often couldn't be there for each other. It's what I was used to, as Lydia had understood.

Still, I couldn't complain about having them around. Tory had done me a favor today, while, as a housemate, Morris tried to be both unobtrusive and useful. He'd dealt with the laundry since Vivien's departure and occasionally ran the vacuum, although I had the impression the noise scared him.

"Maybe the fingerprints will match a known felon or the police will catch a break going door to door around the neighborhood," Tory said. "That necklace is distinctive. They'll check pawnshops and Internet listings, and I'll do the same, to be thorough."

"Much appreciated." No matter how much drama my sister-in-law stirred up in her personal life—there'd been quite a bit recently—she was good at her job.

"Is it okay for me to clean?" Morris asked. "The police didn't leave any of that yellow tape strung around like on TV."

"They don't normally do that in a burglary," Tory said.

"I don't expect you to scrub the place. You're a busy man," I told her father. Except for a young woman he paid to assist in preparing and delivering the catered meals, he did most of the cooking himself. "We need a new housekeeper."

Morris brightened. "I've saved the cards those cleaning services drop off." He must have caught my scowl. "But we don't want a bunch of strangers tromping through here. I'll look for a reliable individual. With references."

"Great." I'd had bad experiences with crews that rotated employees. There was an unacceptable level of breakage and misplaced items.

"Cheese blintzes with blueberry sauce on the menu tonight," he added.

"Sounds wonderful."

"I'll fix a salad." Since Tory was staying in a motel, she'd begun joining us for dinner.

They scattered to their tasks. As my mood calmed, I noticed the accordion-style doors ajar on the double-wide closet. This room had once served as my father's home office and held his old files. He'd brought them here after their contents were digitized, storing them in a metal cabinet so ancient we left it unlocked because we'd lost the key.

My father's notes about Malerie might contain observations that hadn't made it into the computerized version, including signs of postpartum psychosis. Unlike the depression referred to as baby blues, postpartum psychosis is a severe, relatively rare condition that could have gone untreated thirty years ago. The symptoms include confusion, obsessive thoughts about the baby, paranoia and delusions, and it can indicate an underlying issue such as bipolar disorder.

The cabinet drawers were neatly labeled in my father's handwriting: A-L and M-Z. Shouldn't be hard to locate Abernathy, I thought, and pulled on the top left drawer. It stuck, then creaked open.

But I wasn't able to find Abernathy. Between Abbott and Abner, right where Malerie's records should have been, there loomed a large gap.

CHAPTER TWO

Diligent searching failed to unearth Malerie's records. When I phoned Vivien, our former housekeeper was horrified to learn of the burglary and swore she'd never opened those cabinets during her years with us.

My father had been too orderly to yank out a file and fail to return it. This had been done by someone else. Had this been the target of the break-in, or was my discovery coincidental? Or had the burglar grabbed the most convenient file, assuming, wrongly, that it contained financial information?

That night, I tossed until the sheets bunched. After straightening them, I sank into dreams of my lost wife and her shimmering necklace.

On Friday morning, I slid my champagne-colored electric car into a charging station in the medical center parking structure. As I walked toward the exit, a man unfolded his lanky body from a familiar car, its bumper displaying a shiny new parking sticker. Oh, hell. When had that psycho secured office space here?

The best word to describe Dr. Jeremiah Quincy Schwartz, OB/GYN, is creepy. I am not in the habit of disparaging my fellow M.D.s, and as far as I could tell, Jeremiah suffered no more lawsuits than the typical doctor. Nor was it any of my business that he acted as if he'd recently arrived from another planet and had to observe the rest of us for clues how to behave.

The problem was that the people he mostly observed were me and, until her death, Lydia. Take his vehicle. Shortly after my wife and I acquired his-and-hers hybrid sedans—mine blue, hers green—Jeremiah bought the identical model, also blue.

He and I met at Harvard Medical School. I was never sure when he set his sights on Lydia, who'd moved to Boston to be near me, taking a graphic design job at an ad agency. Midway through the first year, her mother died in a car crash. Abruptly, my longtime girlfriend withdrew from our relationship, saying she needed space.

It was a shock when she started dating Jeremiah. I couldn't see what they had in common, aside from both being the grandchildren of Holocaust survivors. He wasn't bad looking, I supposed, with thick curly brown hair and a tall, knobby build.

Within a few months, his strangeness wore thin. She broke it off and, later, returned to me.

Despite my hurt, I bore in mind that we'd been a couple since our freshman year in high school. In our early twenties, the separation allowed us both to discover on a more mature level that we belonged together.

When I chose the University of California, Irvine for my residency, so did Jeremiah. After I joined my father's practice in Safe Harbor, he latched onto a practice in a neighboring town. By then, Lydia and I were married. Although she reported running into Jeremiah annoyingly often, he never broke any stalking laws as far as we could tell.

Unable to ignore him, much as I'd have liked to, I nodded politely. He fell into step beside me as we exited the garage.

Four inches taller than my five-feet-eleven, he measured his pace to mine.

My jaw hurt from gritting my teeth. To break the tension, I said, "New office?"

"I have been on the waiting list." Jeremiah spoke in his usual stilted manner, as if English weren't his native language. It was, unless you counted New York as a foreign country.

"Congratulations."

He glanced at my water bottle. "You no longer drink coffee in the morning?" There was a take-out cup in his hand.

"I drink it at home." Truth is, until Morris moved in, I had grabbed breakfast at the café whose logo decorated Jeremiah's cup. Since we hadn't worked in the same building until now, how had he known which place I frequented?

No sense stewing about it. When I used to complain about him imitating me, Lydia said that as long as he was following, I'd always be ahead.

We entered the glassed-in lobby of the six-story medical building, a boxy partner to the graceful hospital next door. When Jeremiah discarded his cup in a trash can, I had to squelch the impulse to snatch it and have it tested for fingerprints. Despite his fixation, I didn't suspect him of breaking into my house. But I'd better never spot a bulge beneath his shirt that resembled a necklace.

We both exited the elevator on the fourth floor and headed in opposite directions. I refused to turn to see if he was staring after me.

In the office, Farrah was reviewing the appointment schedule on her computer. "How'd it go?" she asked. "Any damage?"

Ah, she meant the break-in. I told her about the jewelry and Mrs. Abernathy's missing file. "If you run across it, please inform me immediately."

"Of course." She snapped her fingers. "I meant to tell you. Dr. Schwartz snagged a suite down the hall." Farrah knew pretty much all about my past, since her aunt Selma used to assist my father.

"I ran into him." I tossed my bottle in the recycle bin.

"According to the grapevine, his temp nurse can't stand him." As usual, Farrah kept me apprised of interesting hospital rumors. "He hired a replacement who starts next week. There's a betting pool on how long she'll last."

"She has my sympathy." Enough about Jeremiah. "Has Dr. Levin come in?"

"Any minute."

I thanked her and went to my private office. There were emails about conferences, questions from patients that Farrah couldn't answer, and a message from my brother-in-law. Barry, a urologist, worked in the newly opened second office tower opposite this one. Tory's low-key younger brother was my favorite of Lydia's relatives.

"Heard about the break-in. Anything I can do?" he'd written.

"It's under control." I considered adding a pleasantry such as wishing him a happy Rosh Hashanah, except I could never track exactly when on our calendar the Jewish New Year fell. Usually September but occasionally October, and besides, he was no more an observant Jew than I was a practicing Christian.

I had just hit Send when Isaiah entered. "You looking for me?"

At nearly seventy, my partner still had more black than silver in his hair and only enough wrinkles to add gravitas. Despite or because of the difference in our ages, we got along well. He was a great source of insights gleaned from experience, while he left the microsurgical procedures to me.

I told him about Malerie's claim. He placed her

immediately, since her late husband had been an anesthesiologist.

"Oh, yes, Winston Abernathy's second wife," Isaiah said. "She inherited a bundle when he died. Smart investor, that man. Someone might be yanking her chain to get at her money."

The possibility of trickery seemed far-fetched. "She has two daughters. I presume they'll inherit."

"And a former son-in-law who's a suspect in his wife's murder, if I'm not mistaken." Isaiah took a keen interest in his colleagues' doings. "Well, even if he is a lawyer, I don't see how he could manipulate matters to his advantage by sneaking in a look-alike."

"About the triplets and their birth. Do you recall any details that might not be in the computer?" I asked.

"Such as?"

"Postpartum psychosis?"

Isaiah tapped his foot. "Doesn't ring a bell, but if something occurs to me, I'll pass it along."

After he strolled out, I called Malerie. A patient with unresolved, puzzling symptoms merited a follow-up.

She answered with a chipper, "Hello?"

"It's Eric Darcy," I said. "How are you?"

"You mean have Snow White and the Seven Dwarfs paraded through my house today?" she replied tartly. "No. I stand by what I saw. I had another dream last night. I can't recall the details but it's driving me crazy, like there's a piece I can't fit into the puzzle."

She wasn't the only one. "I talked to Dr. Levin. He wasn't able to shed any light on the subject." I had no intention of mentioning the lost file, which I hoped would simply turn up. "Malerie, if you'd had quadruplets, they would have been witnessed by the entire delivery team."

"People lie," she snapped. "I'll get to the bottom of this, if I have to hire a private detective to do it."

Not my sister-in-law, I hoped. But a search of birth records couldn't hurt. "By the way, do you have other relatives in the area?"

"Whose daughter is a ringer for my triplets? Hardly." She paused. I waited. "People lie," she repeated. "That gives me an idea."

What a relief if she solved the problem herself. "If I can help, feel free to stop by. No appointment necessary."

"I'll be in touch."

It's hard to gauge how long patients will require, and I try to be there for them. As a result, my duties kept me tied up through lunch. I declined Farrah's and Glenda's offers to stay; my staff members deserve to eat in peace. Since Isaiah took a two-hour break, his nurse was available to pinch-hit for an hour.

Stepping into an exam room in midafternoon, I had a peculiar flash that made me wonder if I was too old to be skipping meals. There she sat, the mysterious redhead, gray eyes solemn, mouth twisting in an off-center smile.

Read the face sheet, you idiot. This was no mystery woman. Not only did she have long hair, but I recognized her husband, Fred Jeffers, as he rose from his chair to shake hands.

I greeted him and Danielle Abernathy Jeffers, one of the two surviving triplets. With her vulnerable expression and vivid coloring, Danielle seemed considerably younger than Fred. He had thinning hair and puffy jowls, although he was only thirty, three years her senior.

As a teenager, Danielle had suffered severe pelvic inflammatory disease, leaving scar tissue that damaged her ovaries and tubes. In six years of marriage, she'd undergone several surgeries, resulting in a single conception. The flare of hope had been replaced by anguish when a life-threatening ectopic pregnancy required a complete hysterectomy, ending her chances of carrying a child.

At my suggestion, they'd started attending an infertility group at the hospital to cope with the stress and to consider their next step. "Have you guys reached a decision?"

"Well, it's important to my husband—to us—to have a child who reflects some of our genetic heritage," Danielle said.

"You're going to hire a surrogate?" Financially, that would be a strain for Fred, a computer programmer, and his wife, a sales clerk. But unlike adoption, it would provide a child with the father's DNA, and success rates have been rising.

The couple exchanged glances. "The problem is the cost." Bitterness laced Fred's words. "Considering how eager my mother-in-law's been to have grandchildren and how rich she is, we figured she'd help."

"She won't even loan us the money." Danielle blinked back tears.

"Not a penny. When we asked, she didn't think twice, the old bat." As Fred grew agitated, his voice rose shrilly.

"Fred!"

"Sorry, honey. But she's rolling in it," her husband said. "What's she plan to spend it on, anyway?"

The refusal baffled me, too. True, Malerie had a reputation for being stingy. When she was widowed, she'd cut off her husband's regular donations to hospital-related charities. Yet after the loss of a daughter, surely the prospect of grandchildren would seem especially sweet.

"She claims surrogates are greedy," Danielle said. "Honestly, they more than earn the money!"

"We'd need an egg donor, too," Fred said glumly. "There's another freaking fortune."

Using a separate egg donor has become standard practice,

since a surrogate who also provides the eggs might develop a strong attachment to the baby. Despite California laws upholding surrogacy contracts, those situations can be difficult.

"If a member of the maternal family donated eggs, that would provide a genetic link on both sides," I pointed out. "And lower the cost."

"If Dee Marie were alive and if her asthma didn't interfere, she'd have done it," Danielle said sadly. "As for Doreen..."

"Out of the question," Fred broke in. "She's well aware I don't approve of her life style. Oh, she may be keeping your mother in the dark, but it's obvious Doreen's gay. If she ever set foot inside a church, they'd set her straight, no pun intended."

"You mean, inside *our* church," Danielle corrected. "Anyway, she'd never trust Fred with her eggs."

"Fine with me," he said. "Homosexuality's hereditary, isn't it, doc?"

That was a controversial subject. "A study of twins in the United Kingdom found that identical twin sisters, who share all their DNA, had a higher incidence of both being lesbians than fraternal twins," I began.

"See, honey? I told you it's genetic," Fred announced triumphantly. "You and Dee Marie were identical, and both normal. Doreen's the odd sister out."

"One limited study isn't definitive." Recognizing that no amount of logical discussion was likely to broaden his views, I handed Danielle a card with the name of the hospital's *in vitro* coordinator. "This lady can get you started choosing a surrogate and a donor whenever you're ready."

"It may be a while," Fred told me dourly.

"Mom might change her mind," Danielle said as she rose. "She called and insisted Doreen and I stop by after dinner. She said it's important."

"I hope nothing's wrong," That was as close as I dared venture to asking if Malerie had mentioned any delusions.

Danielle shrugged. "She wants to come clean, but I have no idea about what."

"I wish she'd included me." Fred held the door for his wife. "A married couple should function as a team."

"How did she sound?" I asked.

"Angry," Danielle conceded. "I can't imagine why."

Did Malerie mean to tell them about her alleged quadruplet sighting? If so, she might provide her hostile son-in-law with an excuse to try to declare her mentally incompetent. No wonder she'd excluded him.

Despite the irrational claim, she struck me as more competent than half the people in Safe Harbor. That included a certain doctor of my acquaintance, I thought as I went to review the next patient's information.

CHAPTER THREE

Driving home through the fading daylight, I crested a rise in the boulevard. Far below spread the harbor with its flock of winged sailboats and, beyond, the vast blue of the Pacific. Only an hour's drive south of Los Angeles, Safe Harbor provided anything a person might crave. Including privacy.

My mental noise faded. I lowered my window to admit the salty air and, with a sense of anticipation, turned left onto Harbor Bluff Drive, left again on Sunset Circle. Like an eagle drifting above the world, I homed in on my aerie.

My heart slammed into my ribs.

In the driveway rested a green sedan. *Lydia's home.* Except that my wife was never coming home again.

She'd willed the car to her sister, who'd declined my offer to pay the difference on a trade-in. Despite the pain of seeing it, I couldn't fault Tory for dropping by to straighten out the mess in the studio. With a tick of hope, it occurred to me she might have tracked the necklace.

Pressing the garage opener, I spotted the suitcases left beside the car. Big ones, shabby and mismatched.

Just as I reached the dismaying conclusion that Tory intended to move in, a red sports car zoomed to the curb. My best friend Keith Sparks once told me that cops ticket red sports cars because they appear to be speeding even when they aren't. I suspect it's more a matter of the color's visibility. Regardless, since police don't generally penalize fellow officers, he gets away with it.

He'd wired open the trunk to accommodate an ugly chipped desk, while the tiny rear seat sprouted chair legs. He'd been half-heartedly complaining about the junk Tory left in their apartment after their fiery break-up a few months earlier. Now it was about to become *my* junk.

I pulled into the garage and strode out to meet Keith. In junior high, he'd been the blond jock who ran interference for the geek. I'd been the scrawny kid, not yet shot up to my full height, who explained algebra until he got it. No matter what paths we'd followed since then, we'd kept reconnecting.

His involvement with Tory had been unexpected. They'd attended the same high school, three years apart, without dating. They'd also both graduated from Cal State Long Beach but, again, with no discernible vibes. Nor at Lydia's and my wedding, where he'd served as best man and she'd been maid of honor.

In the detective bureau, an attraction had flared between them. I'd never trusted it, and here I was, about to suffer radiation sickness from the fallout.

I gestured at the furniture. "Why are you aiding and abetting her?"

"It's not my choice, believe me, but I can't refuse to hand over her stuff." Keith favored me with a half-smile that, I'd observed, inspired women to send him drinks in bars. As a detective, he wore a long-sleeved shirt, slacks, a perpetually loosened tie, and a jacket that didn't quite cover the gun. Even without a uniform, he projected masculine cockiness. "She claimed she's providing you with security after your burglary."

"How's she expect to do that when she's gone during the day?" I grumbled.

"You'll have to ask her." He regarded the suitcases. "Damn. I figured once she got fed up with that lousy motel, she'd forgive me."

"You cheated on her. That's hard to forgive."

"She gets me, more than any other woman I ever met," Keith said. "It was a one-night stand. Tory knew it didn't mean squat."

I rolled my eyes.

"Should have known," Keith amended. "Hey, I didn't plan it. I was waiting to interview a witness at the emergency room over at Heights." He meant Heights View Medical Center, a hospital just north of Safe Harbor.

"Spare me the details." Tory had been close-mouthed, and I wasn't the type to pry.

He ignored my request. "There was this hot nurse and this on-call room. I had no idea she'd text me where Tory would see it."

"It's a bad idea to give out your phone number if you're sneaking around." Before he offered an excuse, I added, "And a worse idea to cheat."

"I apologized. And I've done penance these past few months. No women, no nada." Keith took a deep breath. "I'm not used to this touchy-feely stuff. It's like I always manage to say the wrong thing."

No kidding. In the ensuing detonation, my sister-in-law had not only stormed out of their apartment but also left the police department, claiming too many of the good ol' boys sided with Keith. I pictured Tory blazing her way out with a pistol in each hand, Annie-get-your-gun style.

She claimed to have found her true calling by joining a local agency, Fact Hunter Investigations, where she had more autonomy. I'm not convinced she was really suited to police work, although she'd risen to the rank of detective. She'd started out eager to serve the public but grown increasingly irked when people blamed her for not solving crimes instantly, like on a TV show that wraps up cases in an hour. And she'd complained about judges who slapped bad guys on the wrist.

Her break-up with Keith had been the last straw, thrusting her into a whole new life. Unfortunately, it appeared, that life was mine.

"Better send her back to me before she settles in," Keith advised. "You hate loud music and shouting down the stairs. I'll bet she'll hang her bras on the railing, too."

"Would it be that bad?"

"Worse," he said. "Tell her she ought to be big enough to overlook a minor transgression. Especially since I'm really, really sorry."

I decided not to dwell on the "minor transgression" angle. If the guy hadn't figured out by his mid-thirties how to treat a woman, a lecture from me would be a wasted effort. Yet in this matter, our interests were aligned.

"I'd hate to create ill will by kicking her out," I muttered, seeking advice. "She *is* my sister-in-law."

Keith eyed the front door, which was swinging open. "Lay down rules that'll drive her nuts. She can't tolerate being fenced in. Seriously, she's more like me than she's willing to admit."

"It's worth a try." Being sneaky goes against the grain. On the other hand, so does living in turmoil.

Tory swung down the steps with the wide-hipped stride cops adopt to accommodate their tool-and-gun belts. While she hadn't yet obtained a concealed carry permit, old habits died hard.

She stopped, bushy hair blazing around her face. At five-ten, she'd loomed over Lydia's five-three. Still, no one meeting them had doubted which was the big sister.

For an instant, when she spotted Keith, her mouth quivered. Pain, I thought. But she squelched d it fast. "You boys having fun?"

"Lots to talk about," said Keith.

"Find the jewelry?" I asked.

A shadow crossed Tory's face—literally, from a cloud. "Not yet." Down the short walkway she strode. "Keith, it's the rear upstairs bedroom. Turn right at the top. And don't bang the desk."

"Yeah, it's real delicate."

"I don't care about the desk. The house is a little higher class than you're used to."

Keith shot me an over-to-you expression. *Now or never.* "Tory, I appreciate your concern about security," I began, "but since you're gone during the day…"

"My hours aren't as a predictable as yours." Ruefully, she added, "And the motel's expensive."

"Don't you get paid?" Keith demanded. "Come on, babe. You ditched a steady income loaded with benefits. The least they can do is compensate you fairly."

"I put in ten years, so I'm vested in the retirement plan," she retorted. "Right now I only make a modest salary plus commissions, but I'll start bringing in new clients soon." Most of her assignments, according to Morris, involved rooting out insurance fraud, spying on unfaithful spouses—that ought to appeal to her—and digging up evidence for attorneys in court cases.

Seizing her suitcases, she marched toward the porch. "Another minute and it'll be too late," Keith remarked in my direction.

"Tory!" My voice stopped her on the steps. The luggage

clunked down.

"Yes?"

"The desk." I pointed to the offending item jutting from Keith's trunk. "There's nowhere to put it."

She drew a breath, preparing to argue.

"The décor stays the way it is," I said. "That's one of my rules."

Tory grimaced. To her ex-boyfriend, she said, "You can keep the desk."

"Gee, thanks."

"Also, no loud music, videogames or TV," I improvised.

"I'll use earphones." She'd always disliked earphones. *Think hard.* "No food outside the kitchen."

"You're kidding." From the doorway, Tory regarded me dubiously.

"We have an ant problem," I said. Well, it *had* happened.

"I can live with that." She sighed. "What else?"

I drew a blank. I refused to cite hanging underwear on the railing. "Guess not."

Keith groaned.

I strode up and took hold of a bag. No sense acting churlish. Or should I say, more churlish.

Inside, the scents of tomatoes, cheese, garlic, cinnamon, oregano and cloves swept over me. Even when Morris didn't cook on the premises, he brought hot boxes full of the delicacies he'd prepared for his clients.

The glass had been swept from beneath the taped-up window, I noticed as we crossed the entry hall, which, past the stairs, opens into a great room. After ordering Keith to stay behind, Tory ascended the curving staircase ahead of me.

High above, the skylight bathed the house with end-of-day shimmer. It picked out hues of pearl, blue-green and pink in wall hangings and a small stained-glass window on the landing, as if we were inside an opal.

When Lydia and I accepted Dad's invitation to move in, the place hadn't been updated in twenty years. Provided with free rein and a reasonable budget, my artist wife had spent months designing a color scheme, replacing floors and fashioning custom window coverings. In the process, she'd transformed a house of dark memories into a fairy-tale palace.

I didn't begrudge her sister a chance to stay here. I just loathed the prospect of being startled every night by Lydia's car and wrenched by hearing a voice that, at unexpected moments, eerily resembled hers.

Head low, I trudged into the corner room and found the floor already piled with boxes. My wife used to sleep here if she felt ill or restless, and when I set the case on the bedspread, a hint of her perfume drifted up like a whiff of roses from the garden below.

It wasn't a single blow. It was a flood of memories drowning me in endless pain.

From the window, Tory swung around, tears glimmering. "Being here makes me feel close to her," she said. "I miss her so much."

My self-pity converted into guilt. "I forget that she left other people behind, too."

My sister-in-law squared her shoulders as if embarrassed by her display of emotion. "I hit half a dozen pawnshops and checked online today. No luck but I'll keep at it."

"I appreciate that." Standing aside, I let her go down to dinner. The prospect of Morris's cuisine escorted me the rest of the way to normality.

Although Keith tended to bare his teeth at the prospect of a meatless meal, he joined us for a menu starring Morris's tofu moussaka. I used to give vegetarian food only grudging respect, but my father-in-law had won me over. For the most part.

On the side, there was a green salad, a wild-rice dish and, because it was Friday, the traditional Jewish braided bread called challah. Untraditionally, it was gluten-free, baked with rice flour.

Since Morris had set out candles, Tory lit them and recited a prayer in Hebrew. I'm not sure it was the right one—shouldn't there have been wine to go with it?—but apparently it satisfied her father.

In the kitchen, which is separated from the great room by a free-standing counter, the four of us pulled chairs to the butcher-block table. Ignoring cabinets full of china, we served ourselves on paper plates.

"How's your new delivery girl?" Tory asked her father after we'd finished complimenting him on the meal. "Her name's Billie, right?"

He nodded. "I was a little worried how the clients would react."

"Why?" I looked for a bread knife to slice the challah. Oh, right, we were supposed to tear off chunks. Also, Lydia used to say a separate prayer over the bread, but who was I to complain?

"Purple hair, multiple piercings," Tory answered.

Keith quit shoveling in food long enough to ask, "Why'd you hire her?"

"Her brother's a client," Morris said. "He recommended her. And she's doing well. Last night she made the deliveries by herself with no problems."

"Dad's good with employees." Tory aimed a tongful of salad at her plate. She snatched up the bits that landed on the table.

"Why's that?" Keith mumbled through a mouthful.

"I'm fond of people," Morris said. "You and my daughter see the worst in people, but I see the best."

"Tell Eric about the housekeeper," Tory put in.

"You hired someone?" That had been fast.

"A nice lady named Sandy Faye Miller," Morris said. "She was working for a lady in the next block and dropped in on her lunch break."

"References?" I asked. My father-in-law hadn't exaggerated about seeing the best in people. I was more cautious.

"Yes. I checked them," he said. "In addition to Mrs. Jarvis around the corner, she cleans for Mr. Tran. He works at that flower shop near the hospital. We coordinate with them on special events."

"I see." As he detailed the housekeeper's background, my thoughts wandered. I pictured Danielle Jeffers, who'd soon be meeting with her sister and mother. Perhaps she was already listening to the tale of the mythical quadruplet. What did she make of it?

Abruptly, I snapped to attention. "I beg your pardon?"

Three faces regarded me. "About what?" Keith asked.

"I missed what Morris was saying. Who else does the housekeeper work for?"

"Mrs. Abernathy," he said.

Today, all roads led to Malerie. I got a bad feeling, as if this were an omen. What was wrong with me? I'd never been superstitious.

"Sandy insisted on tidying up the front room," my father-in-law continued. "She hated to leave us with a mess over the weekend. I hired her to start Monday. She's on probation pending your approval, of course."

"I hope she's discreet." I'd hate for my household business to become common gossip.

"She didn't strike me as a chatterbox," Morris said. "And she charges the same as Vivien."

"Good. Thanks for handling this."

The conversation progressed to another topic. Morris had

polled his clients about whether to serve turkey for Thanksgiving this year, and been surprised how many of the vegetarians said yes. "I'll offer a tofurkey option, of course," he said. "But to many people, traditional foods mean a lot."

"Even if it involves the cruel slaughter of defenseless animals?" Keith mocked.

"You're all heart," Tory muttered.

"Nothing spells 'family' like a holiday meal with all the trimmings," Morris said.

I ignored his wistful glance in my direction. Last year, after Lydia's death, I'd been in no mood to give thanks, and I'd already put my foot down about this year. They could eat whatever and wherever else they chose, but I refused to pretend I still had a family.

When Morris's phone played the opening bars of "That's Amore," he tilted his head apologetically and glanced at the screen. "Gotta take this." He answered, "Hi, Billie. How's it going?"

His thick, salt-and-pepper eyebrows drew together. "Slow down. What?" Then, "Did you call the police?"

My stomach tightened. Keith pushed back his chair. Tory drummed her fingers on the table.

"Sure, I can finish the deliveries," Morris said. "Just describe what you saw. Don't worry. You've done nothing wrong." He ended the call.

"What?" we all demanded.

My father-in-law shook his head in disbelief. "She found one of our clients face-down in her swimming pool. Billie thinks she drowned."

No, no, no.

"Who is it?" Tory asked.

In defiance of common sense, I already knew.

"Malerie Abernathy," Morris said.

CHAPTER FOUR

The flashing lights of a patrol car and a paramedic unit flickered across Malerie's house, which appeared almost colorless in the early gloom. Located in the northern part of town, the single-story structure would only have passed muster as a millionaire's home to those familiar with Southern California's sky-scraping real estate prices.

As I drove up, someone switched on floodlights. They illuminated stone facing, a picture window and a giant camellia bush that reached the edge of the steeply pitched roof. The side gate was ajar.

Emergency vehicles and a Golden Fine Foods van jammed the curb. Beside me, Morris pointed to the adjacent corner park. "There's a public lot over there."

"What's wrong with this space?" The wheel responded smoothly beneath my hands as we eased into a tight opening.

"You have great depth perception." Behind me, Tory unsnapped her seat belt. "You'd ace the driving course at the police academy."

"I'll bear that in mind." I hoped I sounded calmer than I felt. My stomach had been churning the whole way over.

The three of us had barely paused to cover the food and set

the alarm. Keith had whipped out his phone, and I'd caught the words "Sergeant? Sorry to disturb you, sir, but..." before he raced outside. He must have persuaded his superior to approve the assignment, because I spotted his red car behind a patrol unit.

Why would they need a detective for a simple drowning? But—chilling thought—Dee Marie's death six months earlier had appeared accidental, too.

On the sidewalk, we joined a knot of neighbors held at bay by a uniformed officer. Above us on a sloping lawn, a middle-aged woman with pinkish hair signaled to me. I recognized Ada Humphreys, owner of the local toy shop.

"Dr. Darcy." She gestured us closer. "Any idea what this is about?"

I described Billie's discovery of the client floating in her pool. "That's all I know."

"Oh, dear. Malerie's in the habit of doing laps before dinner," Ada told me. "When I warned her not to swim alone, she said it was for exercise. I'd have liked to keep an eye on her, but..." She indicated the five-foot fence separating their properties. Ada was too short to see over it easily.

"Swimming's good for lowering blood pressure." I cringed at the realization that Malerie might have read that in one of our brochures.

"Did you observe anything unusual tonight?" Tory asked.

Ada considered. "Now that you mention it, a couple of hours ago I heard raised voices outside, in the back. Malerie sounded furious."

"Did you recognize the other person or pick up what they said?" Tory asked.

"It was a woman, but other than that, no," Ada said. "My hearing's not as good as it used to be."

"Be sure to tell the police about the argument," Tory said.

"Of course."

On the street, the catering van pulled away from the curb. Morris, who had his own set of keys, must have decided not to let the food grow cold while he waited for permission. "Is he going to be in trouble with the police?" I asked Tory. "I mean, since Billie was driving it, and she discovered the... victim." The cruelly impersonal word stuck in my mouth.

"I'm sure they'd prefer to search it, but Dad's worried about his other customers. Unless they have a warrant, he's not obligated to stick around." She shifted uneasily. "Damn. I hate just standing here."

"Miss being in the middle of the action?" I asked.

"I'm not even sure where the middle of the action is any more." In the patchy light, my sister-in-law's usually expressive face was masked.

"Dr. Darcy!" I heard my name, and again, "Dr. Darcy!" Two young women excused their way through the throng, their flowing red hair unmistakable even in a sepia-toned world. "Is Mom hurt? Why are the police here?" Hard to tell whether it was Doreen or Danielle who spoke.

It wasn't my place to tell them their mother might be dead. "She was found floating in her swimming pool. Beyond that, I'm as much in the dark as you are."

"We tried to get past that policeman but he shooed us away," Danielle said. "Can you talk to him?"

Surely the man hadn't realized they were Malerie's daughters. He still wouldn't have admitted them to the house, though, in case it was a crime scene, as I'd learned from watching TV cop shows with Keith, who scoffed at the inaccuracies. Instead, he'd have isolated them—sensible police practice, but harsh in their emotional state. "It might be best not to interrupt the paramedics."

"I just talked to her this afternoon." Doreen's voice

trembled. Slightly heavier than her sister and with broader features, she was an R.N. at Heights. Although she must often face difficult situations with patients, now she was almost pleading for reassurance. "She told us to stop by after dinner for a big announcement."

"She isn't sick, is she?" Danielle regarded me wide-eyed, approaching meltdown. "Is that why she called us here?"

"Her health's fine." I wasn't sure how much I could say without prejudicing their testimony. And why destroy their hope? Maybe the paramedics *would* resuscitate Malerie. "She didn't drop any hints about this announcement?"

Doreen thrust her hands into her jeans pockets. "I thought it might concern her will. She'd talked about changing it."

"She did?" Danielle challenged. "She never mentioned it to me."

"That was a few months ago."

"Pardon me for butting in." Tory's patience had obviously reached its limit. She'd been frowning at me, which I'd ignored. "You guys shouldn't talk among yourselves until the police debrief you."

"What do you mean, debrief us?" Danielle asked.

"Who're you?" Doreen demanded.

I introduced Tory. They both seemed appeased on learning she was my sister-in-law. Then Danielle clapped her hands. "Mom must be all right! The paramedics are leaving."

Yes, they were, without a patient. Not a good sign.

"Let's go in," Doreen said. "I'll tell that policeman…"

"Oh, God." Her sister grabbed her arm.

Into the spot vacated by the paramedics slid a sheriff's sedan. A stocky, uniformed man emerged and fetched a large utility pack.

Danielle gasped. "He's from the Coroner's Office! I've seen him before. He spoke to us at Heights once about his duties."

Danielle uttered small shriek. Shuddering, she leaned against her sister.

Around us, neighbors stopped talking. After a shocked moment, they started up again.

"Oh, dear," Ada said from her porch. "My condolences."

Malerie's daughters shouldn't be learning of her death amid a clump of bystanders. "Let's not jump to conclusions," I said, as if there could be any other reason for the coroner to be there. In my phone, I pressed Keith's number.

"Yeah, what?" came his voice.

"It's Eric." As if he couldn't read my name on his screen.

"I'm busy," growled my friend, in full homicide detective mode.

"You might be interested to learn that Mrs. Abernathy's daughters are out here with Tory and me," I said. "Also that one of the neighbors heard her arguing with someone earlier."

"Oh, hell! I told the patrolmen to separate the witnesses." He clicked off.

Beside me, Danielle was sobbing. "First Dee Marie, now Mom!"

"I can't believe it." Doreen hugged her sister. She was shaking, too.

"Please come inside and sit down," Ada said.

"Hold on a sec." I indicated Keith stalking out of Malerie's house. "That's the detective."

After pausing for a sharp word with a couple of uniformed officers, he approached us, accompanied by the coroner's deputy, whom he introduced. They spoke with the sisters quietly and, when Mrs. Humphreys repeated her invitation, accompanied them into her house.

That left me with Tory. "Do you see Billie?" she asked. "Dad was worried about her. This must be a shock."

I nodded toward a police cruiser where a purple-haired

young woman occupied the front with the door open. "About to be questioned, I guess."

"When no one answered the bell, maybe she peeked over the fence," Tory said. "Since she'd been assisting Dad with deliveries, she might have figured Mrs. Abernathy went for a swim."

"What a disturbing discovery." Reactions to a situation like this can include nightmares or, at a minimum, an intensified awareness of the fragility of life.

Into the welter of vehicles on the street angled a police crime-scene unit. "Keith's treating this as a homicide," I surmised.

"She was murdered?" A man in a jogging suit stared at me. "I thought she drowned."

Tory regarded him coolly. "Do you have information to contribute aside from gossip?"

He ducked his head. Well, we had nothing to contribute either, I thought. Since we'd accomplished our mission of delivering Morris to his van, perhaps we ought to leave. Yet I felt as if I had unfinished business.

My sister-in-law appeared riveted by the movements of the emergency personnel. She'd spent seven years in uniform and three years in crimes against property. Despite her claim that she was happy doing private security work, I feared she'd abandoned her career too readily after her breakup.

A saying of my mother's surfaced: *Don't throw out the baby with the bath water.* Dad used to laugh about that. *Good advice for an obstetrician, wouldn't you say?*

"You know the best part of being a cop?" Tory reflected. "Getting outside my own head. When I was on the job, it wasn't me personally, it was the badge, the sworn oath and the procedures."

Having grown up planning to be a doctor like my father, I'd

never separated my personal from my professional identity. "Is it different as a PI?"

"Yes, maybe because I'm new. Once I start bringing in clients, I'm sure I'll get my feet on the ground. So far I've only worked the cases they assign me."

Minutes ticked by. Like the other bystanders, we awaited enlightenment, or at least an update. As if this were a hospital and the doctor would soon emerge to tell us how the patient was doing.

Keith exited Ada's house and caught my eye. When Tory trailed me, he raised a hand like a traffic cop, halting her. I saw her stiffen, and wondered why he didn't grasp that insensitivity in one situation affected her overall response to him. I doubted he'd welcome the tip, though.

"Are Doreen and Danielle all right?" I asked him.

"They're holding up." From inside his jacket, Keith produced a plastic evidence bag containing a prescription medicine vial. The label belonged to the pharmacy in my building, and the physician's name on it was mine.

"What's this for?" he demanded.

"High blood pressure."

A couple of neighbors edged toward us with curious glances. Tory spread her arms to hold them at bay.

"Could it cause unconsciousness?" Keith asked.

Although surely the coroner's deputy had already filled him in, I understood his technique. In searching for a tricky diagnosis, I often rephrase a question in hopes of shedding new light on the symptoms.

"It happens," I said. "But BP meds aren't sedatives. Hold it higher." When he complied, I studied the bottle. "It's nearly empty. The label indicates it was refilled last week."

"I noticed that," he said.

"If she took all those, it could cause a sharp drop in blood pressure. And yes, she might faint." I hated to think my prescription had contributed to Malerie's death.

Keith tucked away the evidence bag. "We'll have to wait for an official cause of death, but it appears to be drowning, possibly as a result of an overdose of this stuff. Could she have taken them by accident?"

"Older people can become confused and take too many meds," I said. "But she was only sixty. And that's a lot of pills."

"Might it have been deliberate?" His tone remained flat.

"She didn't strike me as a person planning suicide," I replied. "For instance, she asked her daughters to meet her this evening. She didn't say why, except it was important. I doubt she meant for them to find her body."

He didn't react. Danielle and Doreen must already have told him the story. "Did you talk to her recently?"

Out of habit, I hesitated. However, the privacy protections mandated by federal law don't apply during a criminal investigation. And definitely not when the patient might have been murdered.

I explained about Malerie's visit the previous day and her sighting of a woman identical to her daughters. "She insisted there was a fourth baby, a quadruplet."

"Is that possible?"

"It's beyond far-fetched," I said. "Basically, no."

"Was she delusional?"

"I hadn't formed a medical opinion on that score." It occurred to me that I ought to mention the missing file, so I did.

Keith was taking notes so fast I expected his hand to cramp. "Whoever broke into your house stole her file?"

"I'm not sure," I admitted. "I haven't had any reason to look in those cabinets since we digitized."

"When was that?"

"Before Dad died. Over three years ago."

More jotting. "I'll make certain we fingerprint them," he said. "Thoroughly."

Had a killer broken into my house in order to swipe the file, and seized my wife's necklace simply because it was there? Fruitless to speculate.

"The file might surface," I said. "But it's a big coincidence."

"There are way too many coincidences." Keith's nostrils flared. "Starting with someone smothering her daughter."

Dee Marie had been a sweet-natured homemaker. It was widely speculated that the police suspected her husband. Although witnesses placed him at his law office on the afternoon she died, it was only a few miles away. Also, killers can be hired.

When she and her spouse, Rafe Tibbets, had consulted me about the impact of asthma on a potential pregnancy, he'd acted protective toward her. They'd both been pleased to learn that, with treatment and monitoring, her disease shouldn't endanger mother or baby. Why would he have wanted her dead?

Tonight, my main concern was her sisters. If possible, I'd have liked to spare them unnecessary stress. "Do her daughters have to identify the body?"

"No. We found Mrs. Abernathy's driver's license, along with other identification," Keith said.

"By the way," I added, "Doreen indicated her mother might have been changing her will."

"I'll look for a copy." Beyond that, he remained tight-lipped.

The coroner's deputy emerged from Ada's house and headed back toward Malerie's. There was, I had learned from Keith in the past, an overlap in their responsibilities to investigate, interview witnesses and safeguard the scene and evidence.

"I'm sure I'll have questions for you later, but you don't

have to hang around tonight." Keith started off.

Nothing more? My lungs squeezed at the prospect of leaving Malerie without a word of farewell. Or an apology.

"May I view her body?"

"Why?"

"I'm worried I've left out part of what she and I discussed yesterday," I said. "Seeing her might jog my memory."

He shrugged. "Can't hurt. Follow me. Just you."

Tory stood close enough to have been listening. Expression blank, she remained in place.

Keith led me to the far side of Malerie's property, where it adjoined the park. A uniformed officer had cleared a small area, but beyond the crime scene tape, a handful of people were craning their necks toward the fence. One woman held up a cell phone attached to a selfie stick.

"Confiscate that." Keith made a subtle stop gesture toward the cop, which I interpreted to mean he didn't plan to actually do it.

"No way!" The woman fumbled with the stick and nearly dropped the apparatus.

"Well, ma'am, that could be important evidence. We'll return it once we've removed the pictures." Still deadpan, he added, "Unless it gets lost in the evidence room."

Clutching her cell, the woman took off running. The rest of the onlookers dispersed as well.

"That ought to scare the buzzards for now. For Pete's sake, expand the perimeter," Keith told the uniform, and gestured me to the fence. "Let's get this over with."

Bracing myself, I peered into the yard.

A sweep of glowing azure water dominated a pocket paradise. From the kidney-shaped pool and round spa, large flagstones led to a covered outdoor kitchen fitted with stainless steel appliances. I pictured Malerie and her late husband lounging at the glass table, entertaining friends.

The coroner's deputy and several crime scene personnel blocked the huddled figure on the deck. Then a photographer moved aside, yielding a view of Malerie lying on her back, where the paramedics must have placed her. In the glare of floodlights, her dyed red curls stood out against her pale skin and one-piece swimsuit. She looked vulnerable and abandoned.

As a doctor, I'd been in the presence of death before. It's not as if I were an oncologist, though; relatively few patients died on my watch. Still, it happened, and I'd learned to compartmentalize sorrow by reminding myself that I'd done my best to save them.

But Malerie hadn't been sick. Unless the autopsy revealed a stroke or heart attack, nature hadn't killed her.

She'd asked for my help. A fat lot of good I'd done.

"Well?" Keith said.

I could hardly tell him I believed I had a sacred duty to solve this murder. "When I talked to her on the phone this morning..."

"You talked to the victim today?" he snapped. "You didn't mention that."

"Quit interrupting the witness."

"All right," he conceded. "Continue."

"She repeated the words, `People lie,' as if it were significant," I told him. "Spotting a woman who was a dead ringer for her girls—could someone have been manipulating her?"

"One of her daughters?" he prompted.

"Or another relative." I shook my head, unable to dredge up a reasonable speculation. "I have a gut feeling that the quadruplet business is a key, but I haven't figured out what door it opens."

"We're being metaphorical here?" Keith asked. "About keys and doors?"

"Right."

His nostrils flared. He hated metaphors. "Any other ideas?"

"Afraid not."

"Done here." He walked off, and I returned to Ada's lawn.

If I'd expected an epiphany at the sight of Malerie's body, I'd have been disappointed. But I'd received something else: a mission.

My patient depended on me. Not that I imagined I could outsmart Keith and his trained colleagues, but I brought a different perspective. People trusted me, and witnesses might be more willing to open up to a doctor.

No telling where that would lead.

CHAPTER FIVE

The floodlights cast long shadows of three women standing in an uneasy knot on Ada's lawn. At five-ten, Tory towered over the Abernathy sisters and, despite her lower position, her shadow extended beyond theirs.

"I hate that they're holding onto Mom," I heard Danielle say as I returned. She hugged herself, shivering in her light sweater. Due to Southern California's dry climate, temperatures fall rapidly after sunset. "That coroner said it might be next week before she's released."

"Before *her body* is released, is how he put it," Doreen ground out. "What a way to refer to Mom."

Her grief had found release in anger. As for Danielle, her face was splotchy from weeping.

"Today is Friday," I pointed out. "Next week could mean Monday or Tuesday."

"Did he ask you to designate a mortuary?" Tory asked. "That could prevent unnecessary delay."

Doreen tilted her head. "I suggested the Oahu Lane Funeral Home. Mom picked it for Dee Marie's arrangements."

"It's near the animal shelter," Danielle noted. "Mom enjoyed volunteering there."

"I hope she isn't leaving them all her money." Doreen waved away her comment. "She wouldn't do that to us."

Danielle stared at her sister. "Why do you keep suggesting she was changing her will?"

"She summoned us to discuss something important, right?" Her sister had deflected rather than answering, I noticed.

If Malerie *had* meant to change her beneficiaries, that could have provided a motive for murder, but by whom?

Suddenly Danielle emitted a shriek. "You rat! Heather's an estate attorney and Mom knew she was your housemate. She asked if you'd recommend Heather to revise her will, didn't she? And you didn't tell me!"

Heather and Doreen were in a relationship, I'd gathered from Fred's comments in my office. But Malerie supposedly hadn't been aware of that.

Her sister apologized. "Mom swore me to secrecy. She didn't want word getting out to anyone else. Like Rafe, I suppose."

Rafe was also an estate-planning attorney, and had probably drawn up his mother-in-law's old will. With him a suspect in Dee Marie's murder, no wonder Malerie had gone elsewhere, but why keep it secret?

"Why would she trust you and not me?" Danielle asked.

"All I did was confirm that Heather is reliable," her sister said. "I have no clue what they discussed."

"I don't suppose you bothered to tell Mom the truth about you two."

"It wasn't relevant," returned her red-haired sibling. "For your information, I hated keeping secrets from her. Now she's dead and she'll never have a chance to accept me the way I am."

"Or reject you. Was that what you were afraid of?" Danielle was growing agitated. "She refused to help Fred and me pay for a surrogate. Did Heather discuss that with her?"

"I told you, I don't know."

Grief can intensify insecurities and tear families apart; I've seen it right in the hospital. Malerie wouldn't want her daughters to become enemies, and neither did I.

"You've lost your mother and you're both upset," I said. "But her will might not have been what she called you here to discuss."

That stopped the fighting. "You said she wasn't sick," Doreen reminded me.

"True." Here, I realized, was a chance to probe Malerie's state of mind. *Gently.* "Had she mentioned any unusual experiences recently?"

Matching frowns wrinkled their foreheads. "Unusual how?" Danielle asked.

I didn't want to imply their mother had been hallucinating or suffering from dementia. The daughters were distressed enough already. "Such as seeing a familiar person she couldn't place?"

"Not to me," Danielle said. Doreen shook her head, too.

"Dwelling on old memories more than usual?" I prompted.

"After Dee Marie died, sure," Doreen said. "She started leafing through her photo albums."

"Mom wasn't the sentimental type," Danielle added. "But the last six months, we all felt this huge void."

That line of inquiry was leading nowhere. Yet the effort hadn't been wasted. In trying to reach a diagnosis, it can be useful to identify which symptoms *aren't* present.

Across the lawn, Keith spoke to a uniformed officer before vanishing into the house. The young fellow swung through the onlookers, announcing, "Move on, folks! Clear the area." Stomping toward us, he waved his arms. "Let's go, people. You're trespassing on the neighbor's property."

"We have the homeowner's permission, George," Tory said.

"You're a civilian," the cop replied. "The detective ordered us to clear the area, and that includes you." Off he went.

"He has no right to order us off someone else's property as long as we aren't interfering in an investigation," Tory grumbled. "Not worth fighting about it, though."

Judging by the guy's smug attitude, he enjoyed pushing Tory around. I hated bullies. Since I hated getting arrested even more, I held my peace.

The four of us ambled grumpily toward the street. The daughters' annoyance focused on the police.

"They'll blame us because we stand to inherit," Danielle said. "It's the easy way out, right?"

"Yeah, they did such a great job of catching whoever killed Dee Marie," Doreen agreed. "Not that I'm a fan of Rafe's, but if he did it, they should have charged him by now."

"The district attorney files charges, not the police," Tory said. "Still, it's frustrating that they haven't made an arrest." In the past, she'd have defended her fellow officers.

"I hate being told to go home and wait. For what?" Doreen said.

"For them to point fingers at us," finished her sister.

We reached the sidewalk, about to go our separate ways. *As long as you're sticking your nose in other people's business, Eric, might as well go the whole nine yards.* "Danielle, Doreen." Both halted. "Have you considered hiring a private investigator?" I asked. "You have an excellent one right here."

Tory's spine stiffened. Well, she'd claimed she needed clients. If she wasn't happy with my meddling, she should have been more careful what she wished for.

"You know," Doreen said, "that isn't a bad idea."

*

Although Safe Harbor Medical employs obstetricians to

supervise the night shifts in Labor and Delivery, complications can arise. When necessary, the patient's attending physician is summoned, and thus the charge nurse awakened me shortly before 5 a.m. on Saturday.

After a night of vague, disturbing dreams, it was a relief to immerse myself in the details of obstetrical care. One breech birth resolved without the need for surgery, but several cesarian sections followed. I never take happy outcomes for granted, and, following the previous day's tragedy, it was particularly gratifying that all mothers survived in good shape and their babies emerged healthy.

When my schedule permitted, I checked on my small patients in the nursery. One little cuddler nestled into my arms, blinking at me with brown eyes beneath a shock of black hair. No matter who he became or what mark he made on the future, I imagined he would never be more purely himself than at this moment.

An ache caught in my throat, like a pill that fails to wash down. Having a child of my own had been a fiercely held dream, one that I'd discovered, belatedly, Lydia didn't share.

I returned the baby to his clear-sided bassinet. This little guy had lots of people to love him. Lucky him. Lucky them.

By one o'clock, I was off duty. Descending from the third floor, I recalled how, last night, Doreen had welcomed my suggestion of hiring Tory. Concerned about the expense, Danielle had bowed out.

Tory had requested permission to discuss her findings with me. "Of course," Doreen had said. "There's nobody I trust more than Dr. Darcy."

Tory had also explained that she had to share pertinent information with the authorities. "I can't interfere with a police investigation."

"Whatever gets us to the truth." Her new client had agreed

to sign a contract as soon as her girlfriend/lawyer reviewed it.

At the hospital, I reached the main floor, where the scents of grilling onions and roasting chicken nearly drew me to the cafeteria. However, experience had shown that no matter how delicious the aromas, the reality of hospital food couldn't compare to whatever Morris might whip up or leave in the refrigerator.

As I veered toward the staff exit, an unwelcome shadow attached itself to my side. Jeremiah never lacked spring in his step, although he'd presumably spent the morning treating patients, too. Dark hair notwithstanding, his jaw rarely sported a stubble of growth, and his clothes were immaculate. Yet he had an ungainly stride, as if he'd been assembled by a beginner.

"It is unfortunate that patient of yours drowned." From his tone, he might have been discussing the weather. "I gather she was murdered."

Had the news media picked up on Malerie's death? "Where'd you hear that?"

"The cafeteria is amazing." Moving ahead, Jeremiah held the door for me. I muttered my thanks. "You can receive a complete news report without trying."

"Another good reason for eating at home," I observed as we cut across a small reserved lot.

"Did you know that Mrs. Abernathy used to work here?" he asked.

That startled me. How embarrassing. Malerie had been my father's patient and then mine, but it took Jeremiah to provide this vital background. "No, I didn't."

"A nurse's aide," he said as we passed the office building. "Back when it was a community hospital. Someone said that is how she met her husband. He was an anesthesiologist."

"I'm aware of that." I recalled Winston Abernathy as a crusty but decent fellow, not that we'd been well acquainted.

He'd died shortly after I joined Dad's practice four years ago.

I wished my father were here to fill in the blanks. However, I was stuck with Jeremiah as a source.

"She assisted with his care after he was injured in a car crash." Jeremiah shortened his stride when it threatened to carry him ahead of me. "That was how his wife died. In the crash. He was driving. Then Mrs. Abernathy swooped in. But she was not Mrs. Abernathy yet."

"Swooped in?" It struck me as a judgmental term.

"I am only repeating what I heard," he replied. "People believe they were having an affair before that, during his marriage. Then they broke up for a while, if I followed the sequence correctly."

"Considering that this happened thirty years ago, it's second or third hand gossip at best." And an unkind way to talk about a dead woman.

"There are still personnel on staff from those days." Jeremiah didn't sound offended.

"True." But why bring up such cruel, old gossip? If the implication of adultery bothered me, I could imagine how it might upset their daughters.

Our footsteps resounded on the concrete floor of the parking structure. There it waited, the blue hybrid like my former one save for the license plates.

"I will be replacing that," Jeremiah commented. "The dealership was out of your shade. They describe it as champagne. I would call it beige."

He discussed this as if it were perfectly normal for him to buy a duplicate of my car, and as if we'd agreed that he should copy my taste in automobiles as well as women. "Maybe you should live dangerously and try another color," I said. "How about silver?"

Oh, hell, why did I pick that one? Silver had been Lydia's

maiden name.

Jeremiah didn't appear to catch the double entendre. "Do you think that would be better? I ordered champagne, but I could cancel it."

"Suit yourself," I told him.

He blinked. "I will stick with champagne."

Why fight it? "Good choice." For the sake of courtesy, I concluded, "Later."

"Later."

Driving home, I wondered what Tory had discovered that morning. Her plans, she'd related over a late-night snack, had been to meet with Doreen and her partner, Heather, and to canvass the neighborhood for witnesses. As she talked, the animation had returned to her face. It felt good to see my sister-in-law energized.

She'd also intended to stop by the detective bureau with a box of doughnuts and mention she was willing to provide whatever information she ran across. Perhaps they'd share with her in return.

At this hour, morning low clouds had burned off to reveal a glorious October afternoon. Ahead, the Pacific Ocean sparkled innocently, as if neither sharks nor riptides lurked beneath its surface.

In my neighborhood, a handful of folks walked dogs or pushed strollers along the sidewalk. Except for a few pairs strolling together, they maintained a distance, as if a film director had instructed them to space their intervals.

Looking forward to peace and quiet, I turned onto my street. But there was no serenity at my house. I heard angry shouting and spotted Keith's red sports car behind a white van bearing a police logo.

Not another break-in, I prayed silently. Please, Lord, not another murder.

CHAPTER SIX

Bloody murder was more like it, judging by my father-in-law's yelling from the porch. Waving a rubber spatula and sporting a red checkered apron that emphasized his rotund form, Morris screamed a single word over and over. "Sanctuary! Sanctuary!"

Behind him stood the rail-thin young woman I'd glimpsed the previous night as she waited to be interviewed. Daylight failed to soften the spiky impression of her purple hair, tattoos and piercings, and her expression indicated her shock had transformed into anger.

After maneuvering around the catering truck in the driveway, I parked and got out. The target of Morris's wrath, Keith stood with arms folded. A crime scene technician, swathed in protective gear as if my house might conceal chemical or biological hazards, hovered on the sidewalk.

Keith's attention shifted to me. "Would you confirm to your father-in-law that we have permission to print the file cabinet?"

"Don't let them in!" Despite his round nose and the puffs of hair above his ears, Morris did not cut a comical figure. Well, okay, maybe a little, but it would have been disrespectful to smile. "It isn't Billie's fault she found Mrs. Abernathy's body. They interviewed her last night. She's told them what she knows."

"Morris, if Keith intended to haul your assistant off to jail, he'd have done it by now," I said.

"They're harassing me." Billie had an unexpectedly throaty voice. "Look at how they've treated my brother."

"Your brother?" I must have missed something.

"Rafe Tibbets," Keith clarified.

Aha. The chief suspect in Dee Marie's murder was also the client who'd recommended Billie to Morris. Now she'd stumbled over, let's see, her brother's former mother-in-law's dead body. I could see why that might arouse a detective's interest.

"Eric authorized us to enter the premises and dust for prints," Keith said.

"That's not what you stated earlier." Morris held his ground with a ferocity I'd never seen in him before. "You have more questions for her."

"A few," Keith admitted. "Issues always come up as we examine the larger picture."

That made sense to me. Also, I wasn't thrilled by this melodrama on my normally serene premises.

"It's a trap!" Billie cried in my direction, as if I'd been elected referee. "They've been trying to pin Dee Marie's murder on Rafe for six months. They're too lazy to track down who really did it. I won't say a word except in front of witnesses."

Keith shook his head. "I need to talk to you privately. Having other people present can taint your testimony, and theirs."

"No." She shrank behind her protector. Not an easy task,

since she and Morris were about the same height, roughly five-foot-six. Still, his weight surpassed hers by a wide margin, literally.

He went on glaring at the detective. "Send in the CSI tech. He can get the prints and leave. And you should go with him."

Keith frowned. "Let me do my job, okay, Morris?"

"Billie works for me and she's here at my invitation." My father-in-law's pudgy face set grimly.

It was a standoff. While the young woman had a right to refuse to talk to the police, this scene accomplished nothing except to draw neighbors onto their porches. That's a rare event on Sunset Circle. The last time I recalled people venturing out en masse—well, en mini-masse—was after an earthquake rattled our dishes.

Hoping to hurry matters along, I indicated the open door. "What's that fantastic aroma?" My stomach rumbled for emphasis.

"Spiced eggplant for sandwiches," said my father-in-law. "We've been experimenting with recipes."

"There are sweet potato fries, too." A fleeting smile transformed Billie into an engaging young woman.

Keith wrinkled his nose. "I'd go for the sweet potato fries, but seriously—eggplant sandwiches?"

"Not everyone can eat peanut butter," Billie snapped. "It's poison to people who're allergic, like my brother."

Keith blew out a frustrated breath. Although I was sure his stomach matched mine growl for growl, he had a murder to solve. Two, including Dee Marie's.

Morris glanced worriedly into the house. "We left the food simmering. I'm afraid it'll burn. Maybe you should talk to Keith."

"Don't abandon me." Billie's hand clamped on his arm.

"Would you like me to hire a lawyer?" I asked. That would

cost a bundle, but we had to break the logjam. "I'm Eric Darcy, by the way."

"Billie Tibbets." She wavered. "I guess you're an objective observer. I'll talk to the cop if you're there, okay?"

"Keith?" I asked.

From his disgruntled expression, I gathered he was weighing the disadvantages of having me listen in vs. waiting for and contending with a lawyer. "All right. How about the game room upstairs?"

"Works for me," I said. Billie gave a short nod.

Inside, I accompanied the technician to the conservatory. On the threshold, as midday light flooded the disarray, my peripheral vision swept over a crumpled shape. For a jolting second, I thought I saw Malerie's body crumpled on the floor.

Keep breathing, Eric. One of Lydia's multicolored capes had tumbled from the clothes rack.

Keith's hand rested on my shoulder. "It must be hard to see this."

"It's as if someone died here." Immediately, I regretted the comment. "I'm sorry. This burglary is minor compared to what happened to Mrs. Abernathy."

"It's natural to feel violated," he said. "Is that the filing cabinet you meant?"

I showed him where Malerie's file should have been, and we left the tech to his task. Morris had vanished into the kitchen, from which drifted the mouth-watering scents I'd caught earlier.

Her spine rigid, Billie followed Keith up the curving stairs and into the game room, which had doubled as my father's library. At Dad's request, the dark woods and high shelves displaying books and memorabilia had remained largely unaltered during Lydia's redecoration. That hadn't precluded the addition of a large TV screen, a videogame system and a parquet table suitable for board games and jigsaw puzzles. Plush armchairs flanked the faux leather sofa.

Billie chose the seat nearest the door, which Keith shut quietly before producing a recorder and notepad. He didn't mention her rights. As Tory had once explained, a Miranda warning is only required when the interviewee's taken into custody.

Into the recorder, Keith introduced himself, stated the time, date and place, and identified those present. A subtle change straightened his shoulders and steadied his voice. In his dozen years on the force, I realized, I'd never seen him at work until now.

After checking his notes, he said, "Miss Tibbets, did you speak to Mrs. Abernathy last night?"

Her chin lifted. "How could I? Like I told you, when no one answered the door, I went to the gate and saw her floating in the pool. I called for help."

"Who did you call first, Mr. Golden or 911?"

"911."

Keith jotted a note. "You didn't arrive earlier? Possibly there was a mix-up with her meal and she sent you to fetch a different one?"

He was, I presumed, trying to establish whether it was Billie the neighbor had heard quarreling with Malerie.

"No." She heaved a breath. "Did you check with the previous customer to confirm when I left her house?"

"She couldn't recall exactly," Keith said. "You never spoke to Mrs. Abernathy at all?"

"We neither whispered, yakked, gabbed, communicated, conversed nor palavered."

He paused, pen in midair. "Excuse me?"

"I have a degree in English literature," she said.

That startled him into blurting, "You don't look it." For a

second, he became a more familiar, less solemn Keith.

"How is an English major supposed to look? Like I'm headed for a Renaissance fair?" Despite the defiant manner, her voice trembled. Was that the result of stumbling across a dead body, or did it indicate guilt?

I wished I could read Billie's mind. Or Keith's.

He produced a polite smile. "No offense intended, Miss Tibbets."

She didn't reply.

Keith shifted on his chair. "Was Mrs. Abernathy a difficult customer?"

"We got along," Billie said.

"Were you acquainted with her outside of work?"

"Yes, obviously," she returned. "I was a bridesmaid at my brother's wedding. To her daughter. The one whose murder you haven't solved."

He ignored the taunt. "After Dee Marie's death, did Mrs. Abernathy blame your brother?"

"You asked me that last night."

"Just seeing if you have anything to add," he said.

"She was wary of him." Billie fidgeted. "In the past, she used to consult him about legal stuff, and she stopped doing that."

"What was her reaction when you first showed up with her meals?"

"She wasn't thrilled about my hair color and my new tats," Billie admitted. "But she told Morris I was a nice girl. Okay? You done interrogating me?"

He fiddled with his pen. Often, people feel compelled to rush into a silence and may spill more than they intended. As the seconds ticked by, my stomach complained, but I kept my mouth shut. Billie kept hers shut, too.

Finally, Keith said, "That's it for now. Thank you."

I wondered what he'd learned. Maybe it's like shaking a

fruit tree that you've already harvested, just to see what else falls out.

When I reached the kitchen, Morris was running the food processor. "Done? Good. It's lucky we came inside or I'd have burned lunch," he said. "And that's practically a crime in itself."

From the assortment of dirty dishes and pots, I gathered this was a complicated recipe. I admire cooks who spend hours preparing repasts for others. As a teenager living with my father after Mom died, I'd learned to fix spaghetti, canned soup and packaged macaroni and cheese. As an adult, I could follow a simple recipe but quickly lost patience with long lists of ingredients and procedures. If I put that much effort into an operation, I'd like to at least save somebody's life.

Usually, we ate at the counter or the small kitchen table, but today Morris had set a cheese and relish tray, a basket of bread and small bowls of condiments in the breakfast nook, which overlooks the garden. Billie retrieved crisp julienned sweet potatoes, and my father-in-law served a bowl of eggplant-tomato mixture.

Keith strolled in. "Tech's on his way out," my friend announced.

"You get all the elimination prints you need?" I asked. Police have to identify prints belonging to people who live or work at a crime site to isolate those that don't belong there.

"We should be good. Tory arranged for your old housekeeper to stop by the San Francisco P.D. to be printed." As Keith grabbed a paper plate, he gazed around with a puzzled expression.

"Missing something?" I inquired.

"Tory?" His tone was almost casual.

"Not sure where she's gone," I said. None of us volunteered that she was working on the case.

Keith layered the eggplant mixture on rye, using three

slices interspersed with lettuce, cheese and tomatoes. "My compliments to the chef." He raised his concoction, the type my mother would have called a Dagwood sandwich.

Morris smiled in acknowledgement. Billie stared at her plate.

"Honestly, Miss Tibbets, I don't bite," Keith informed her, right before he took a chomp.

Behind him, Tory snorted. Busy eating, I hadn't noticed when she slipped in, and Keith was facing away from her. I could tell the instant he registered her presence, because the lines of his face softened and his pupils dilated. It's what's termed a micro-expression, a fleeting glimpse of truth beneath the defenses.

He wanted Tory back. If he played his cards right, he might still have a chance with her, I thought with a flicker of hope. Much as I liked my sister-in-law, I'd rather she left. The rustlings in the night and the whiff of scents with which toiletry manufacturers douse their products served as unwelcome reminders of my wife's absence.

"Where've you been?" Keith asked.

"Investigating a case for a client." Tory pulled out a chair. Billie, who'd consumed only a few olives, seized on the interruption to flee to the clean-up area.

"Which case?" Keith queried.

Tory sighed. "Mrs. Abernathy's." Anticipating trouble, she added, "A second set of eyes never hurts, right?"

"You were a good detective," he conceded.

"Still am."

"Granted," he said. "And your client is?"

"Rather not say."

Keith shrugged. "I saw you on the sidewalk talking to Doreen."

Tory finished assembling her sandwich. "Okay, you got me."

They ate side by side, in sync yet out of sorts. Before splitting up three months ago, they'd lived together for half a year, after an acquaintance that dated back to high school. A bond remained, but it had weakened.

My thoughts turned to the case. "Do you think the same person murdered Mrs. Abernathy and Dee Marie?" Both of them squelched me with a none-of-your-business look. "Hey," I protested to Tory, "I realize Keith can't talk, but *you* could speculate."

"I'd rather deal with facts."

"Right you are," Keith said, and took another bite of his thick sandwich. Eggplant squirted onto his shirt. "Hell."

Tory dipped a wad of paper napkins into his water glass and handed it to him.

"Thanks."

"Don't mention it."

Ducking his head to cover a smile at his daughter's show of domesticity, Morris went to the sink. I heard him thanking Billie, who hugged him before heading off.

Keith finished mopping his shirt, with spotty results. After the front door clicked, he addressed Tory again. "Did Rafe Tibbets speak with you?"

"He declined. Doesn't trust either of us, I guess."

"Interview the daughters?"

"Doreen," she confirmed. "I can't repeat what my client said, but she promised it was the same stuff she told you."

How frustrating. "Doreen did give permission to include me," I pointed out, hoping for a glimmer.

After a pause, Tory said, "Before her death, Dee Marie had been trying to straighten out her mother's papers, which disappeared along with her laptop. Stolen by her killer, presumably."

"So the husband claims," Keith put in.

Was there a connection to my missing file? "What kind of papers?" I asked.

"Business letters, financials and so on," Tory said. "Apparently Mrs. Abernathy was slapdash with her records. Dee Marie quarreled with her mother, but Doreen wasn't sure if it was because of the carelessness or something she stumbled across."

"Any idea what that might have been?" Keith asked.

"Afraid not, but I'll raise it with Danielle," Tory promised. "I'm meeting with her and her husband Monday night."

"Keep me advised?"

"Sure."

Around a mouthful of sandwich, Keith mumbled, "What else'd you do today?"

"Canvassed the neighborhood for witnesses you missed."

"Find any?"

Her curly hair bounced as she shook her head. "I got bupkes."

"Did it hurt?"

She chuckled. "That's Yiddish. It means nothing."

"If it means nothing, why use it?" When he flashed a grin, she poked his arm.

I half expected them to get into a playful tussling match. Then Tory drew back, her expression darkening as if she'd just remembered who else he'd been tussling with.

He'd been an idiot, if you asked me. No one did.

Having finished the sandwich, Keith rose and brushed off crumbs. "You're making the right moves, as I'd expect. Of course, you're at a disadvantage, being in the private sector. Hope you don't find it too discouraging."

"Yeah, poor me." Tory drew herself up to her full height, only a couple of inches shorter than his. "Oh, I did learn they've scheduled a memorial gathering tomorrow afternoon for family and close friends."

"Is Rafe Tibbets invited?"

"Presumably," she said.

"I'd better be there."

Her eyes rounded in mock sympathy. "I'm afraid you're not invited. Feel free to call Doreen but she insisted you won't be allowed inside. She's upset that you haven't solved her sister's murder."

Keith's jaw twitched. DNA samples, omnipresent cameras and computer records provide police with an incredible array of evidence, but they can't compel witnesses to open up to them.

"How about me?" I asked.

Tory smiled. "Doreen expressly invited you, Eric."

"Wouldn't miss it," I said.

In a long ago English class, we were assigned to list adjectives describing a friend. Despite a ban on insults, some leeway was allowed. The words I put down for Keith included determined, energetic and bullheaded. I picked that over stubborn because of the way he lowers his head like a bull about to charge, which he was doing now.

He'd grown older, though, and occasionally wiser. "You'll let me know what you dig up?"

"Naturally," Tory said. "We have the same goal."

Did they, personally as well as professionally? I scooped up platters and headed for the kitchen, leaving them space.

After a murmured exchange, I heard Keith assure her he would do his best not to act like a knucklehead. "As you mentioned, an extra set of eyes comes in handy."

"So does spot remover," she responded lightly. "There's a spray bottle on the shelf with your laundry detergent."

"Thanks."

Their exchange might not qualify as a reconciliation. But to me, it marked a welcome ceasefire.

CHAPTER SEVEN

Tory and I drove to Sunday's gathering in Lydia's old car. Since my initial offer to pay the difference on a trade-in, I hadn't complained about her keeping it, but it was hard to concentrate when stray scents and the sound of the gearshift jerked me into the past. A happier past that faded into darkness around the edges, like an old-fashioned portrait vignette.

Doreen Abernathy and Heather Blythe lived near Safe Harbor Community College. En route, Tory filled me in on her efforts of the previous afternoon. She'd re-interviewed the neighbor and attempted to follow other leads, but was no closer to discovering who'd been arguing with Malerie or why anyone had wanted her and Dee Marie dead.

"The standard advice is to follow the money," she told me. "I'd like to get my hands on Mrs. Abernathy's financials, plus a copy of her will. So far, no luck."

"Did she actually change it?" I asked.

"According to Doreen, Heather hasn't shared the details of what she and Mrs. Abernathy discussed, citing attorney-client privilege." Tory kept her attention on the road. "I'm not sure how that applies once the client is dead. If there's a new will, she'd be obligated to provide copies to the heirs, especially whoever is designated as executor."

I sympathized with a person's right to privacy even in death. However, a part of me wished the universe maintained a repository of all knowledge, for the peace of mind of those who survive. "Anything further about why she invited her daughters over the night she died?"

"Only that she had a big announcement." Tory tapped the steering wheel as we waited at a red light. "Families harbor secrets, don't they?"

"They do." That reminded me of Jeremiah's gossip. "I'm reluctant to repeat rumors…"

"Repeat away."

I relayed the speculation that Malerie and her husband had had an extramarital affair. "That could have scored a few enemies."

"The first wife's dead and they had no children," Tory responded. "Who's left to bear a grudge?"

"It's an interesting rumor."

"Which it would be beyond insensitive to bring up at a memorial."

I had to agree.

We parked a block away and walked to the condo development. The Spanish-style units sported tile roofs and stucco walls, with squatty palm trees and azalea bushes lining the pathways. Tory navigated, since she'd previously interviewed Doreen and her roommate here.

The bell summoned a woman in her late fifties. Dark-blond hair hung loose around her shoulders, setting off pleasant, regular features. My assumption that this was Heather vanished when she introduced herself.

"I'm Sandy Faye Miller." The woman ushered us inside. "I start work for you tomorrow, Dr Darcy."

Aha, the housekeeper Morris had engaged. "You cleaned for Malerie," I recalled.

"Yes, I did." To our right, a sunken living room featured pale woods and geometric paintings, the type Lydia used to say interior designers stocked by the truckload. To the left, a hallway led to what I presumed was the bedroom wing. "Doreen requested that I assist today. Of course, I'm happy to do it. Mal was a friend as well as a client."

"Have the police talked to you?" Tory asked.

If the question startled Sandy, she didn't show it. "Yes, a detective Sparks. I'm afraid I couldn't tell him much. I was working at another client's house on Friday."

Voices and the clink of glassware drew us straight ahead to a glass-roofed atrium. Sunshine filtered through the skylight, bathing ferns and guests in a mellow glow.

A cloth-covered table held trays of hors d'oeuvres, a coffee pot, pitchers of drinks and a couple of wine bottles. About a dozen people stood speaking in tones as somber as their outfits, which ranged from suits to jeans. In Southern California, if your underwear doesn't show, your attire can pass for dressy.

A short woman in a tailored pantsuit cut away from Doreen's side. Despite perilously high heels and the pile of ash-blond hair atop her head, she couldn't have cleared more than five-feet-two. Her manner was far from diminutive, however, as she seized my hand. "I'm Heather Blythe."

"Eric Darcy." I complimented her home and expressed my condolences.

"Thank you. It's been rough."

"Don't waste your sympathy on her." At the refreshment table, Danielle's husband, Fred, was refilling his wine glass. "Glad you're here, Doc. We know *you* really cared about Malerie."

"Like I didn't?" Heather responded irritably.

"Let's be civil, please." Doreen touched her girlfriend's arm. A look passed between them, as if they'd discussed ground rules earlier. To me, Doreen said, "We'll be holding a service shortly, to share memories of Mom. I'd appreciate if you'd say a few words."

"I'd be honored."

"And I can lead us in prayer." Fred addressed his sister-in-law as if daring her to object. "I'll try to make it bland enough not to offend those who'd rather not involve God in their lives."

"Oh, here we go," Heather grumbled.

"I'm sure Malerie would have appreciated everyone's input." Ada Humphreys accompanied her words with a neighborly smile. Running a toy store had sharpened her skills with quarrelsome children, I mused.

Danielle turned to Tory and me. "Have you heard any more about when they might let us have Mom's body? We'd like to plan the funeral."

"The autopsy was conducted yesterday," Tory told her. "The coroner hasn't stated a cause of death pending further tests."

"How long will that take?" Fred asked. "Since you seem to have a private line into information that by rights should belong to all of us." His hostility surprised me.

Tory maintained a professional air. "Could be weeks for the tox report, but they won't need her body that long. The coroner routinely holds the subject for two days post-autopsy."

"Why?" Danielle asked.

"Some conditions such as bruising may not show up until then," Tory said. "Once that period passes, they should release her."

"Miss Golden is a private investigator," Doreen informed the gathering. "She's digging into Mom and Dee Marie's murders on behalf of the family."

"You mean, on behalf of you and your... *friend*," Fred sniped. "You're the ones who hired her."

"If you don't mind my asking, what does a PI do in a case like this?" said a dark-skinned man I recalled from the knot of observers outside Malerie's house. "Can you really uncover evidence the police miss?"

"Occasionally, yes. Or it may be a question of interpreting the evidence differently, bringing a fresh perspective," Tory told him. "Also, witnesses often talk more freely with a PI than with the police." Nor, she'd mentioned previously, were PI's required to read people their rights.

Her remarks drew no comment from Fred. Recalling that they had an interview scheduled for the next evening, I hoped his antagonism was aimed more at Doreen than at her.

"Do you carry a gun?" asked a fellow I guessed to be in his eighties.

Tory shook her head. "I'm trained in firearms but I don't have a carry permit."

"Isn't it unusual, hiring a detective?" commented an elderly woman in a wheelchair. I wondered who she was.

"Attorneys often hire investigators," Heather told her.

"Only when they defend crooks," Fred put in.

"In civil cases as well," Heather answered. "If you were being sued, wouldn't you want all the facts?"

"Well, no one ever sued my brother," the woman announced, although no one had implied otherwise. "Anesthesiologists frequently get dragged to court, but not Winston."

She must, I deduced, be the triplets' aunt on their father's side.

"At least that's what he told *her*," Tory murmured in my ear. We were both aware that almost every doctor gets sued, no matter how careful we are.

"If you don't mind more questions," continued the neighbor who'd shown an interest in PIs, "I'm wondering what there is to investigate. Didn't Malerie drown while swimming alone?"

"There might be more to it," Ada said. "But is this an appropriate topic for her memorial service?"

The aunt ignored her. "I heard she drowned because she overdosed on her medication. You were her doctor, weren't you? What do you think?"

I hadn't expected to be put on the spot. "It's not my place to discuss a patient's medications."

"We're her family, and I'd like to know," Doreen said. "Wouldn't you, Danielle?"

"Yes."

What the hell. I aimed my response at the sisters. "She was on blood pressure pills. An overdose can cause dizziness or sleepiness."

"An overdose? Don't tell me it was suicide!" cried the lady in the wheelchair. Danielle gasped.

"I doubt it." I hurried to clarify. "When I spoke with her by phone Friday morning, she didn't sound depressed, or euphoric either."

"Euphoric?" Heather queried.

"Often when people resolve to kill themselves, they're temporarily relieved and their mood lifts."

As I was contemplating how to steer the conversation away from this subject, Danielle asked, "Could she have swallowed the pills by accident?"

I repeated what I'd told Keith. "It's possible. Older people can become confused about whether they've taken their medication."

Doreen nodded. "Mom did get confused with her paperwork, and her checkbook was a mess. That's why Dee

Marie volunteered to help."

"I think her mental state deteriorated after her hip surgery," added Sandy, who was refilling the pitcher of iced tea. "While I don't believe she had dementia, she could be absent-minded. Still, I'd been living out of state, so maybe the change was gradual."

"Mom hired Sandy to take care of her after the operation," Danielle explained for my benefit. "They used to be nurse's aides together at the hospital."

"We stayed in touch after I moved back to Idaho," Sandy said.

"If you're a nurse's aide, why are you working as a housekeeper?" Tory asked.

"Better hours and less stress," the older woman answered. "Once Mal recuperated, I stayed on part-time. By then I'd found other clients and a convenient place to live."

As an old friend, Sandy would be a good source of information about events surrounding the triplets' births and Malerie's relationship with Dr. Abernathy. "You should interview her," I told Tory quietly.

"Already noted."

"I'd like to begin the service," Doreen announced. "If everyone will set up a folding chair, we can start."

We fetched seats from a stack at the side and arranged them facing a table laid with green cloth, like an altar. A spreading white-and-yellow bouquet covered most of the surface.

The delicate scent recalled the floral tributes that had arrived at my house after Lydia died. There'd been no service in Safe Harbor, however. Under the plans she'd written out before departing, she'd been buried in Israel, where she'd gone to explore her heritage. There, during a visit to the ancient cliff-top fortress of Masada, she'd plunged a thousand feet to her death.

Had it been an accident or intentional? We'd probably never know.

At home, I'd been so distracted that, a few hours after learning of her death, I'd fallen down the stairs, breaking a leg and spraining my shoulder. A psychologist might contend I'd subconsciously mirrored my wife's fatal fall, but I put it down to distraction. Unfortunately, my injuries had prevented me from traveling.

Tory had gone to supervise her sister's burial. In Israel, she'd questioned the authorities and the tour guide. They'd speculated that Lydia's fall resulted from heat exhaustion, since the temperature that day had been over a hundred degrees Fahrenheit.

I'd decided against holding a memorial in Safe Harbor, loathing the prospect of fielding questions and accepting condolences. Morris and Tory had suggested it was a mistake to mourn in solitude, but I'd never been able to draw comfort from anyone except Lydia.

Had she chosen death? Why had she shut me out, those last few months?

Here in the atrium, the speakers' words flowed over me. Danielle read a loving message her mother had written on her and Fred's wedding day, and Doreen drew chuckles with anecdotes about the young triplets driving their mother crazy.

"Our parents weren't perfect, but in retrospect, I realize what a happy childhood we had," she said. "Mom loved and cherished us. She'd have gone to any lengths for her kids."

Nearby, Sandy drew a deep, painful breath. When heads turned toward her, she said, "Mal could be difficult but she was a friend to me when I had no one else."

"Dr. Darcy?" Doreen prompted.

Recalling her earlier request, I summoned a few words

about Malerie's peppery personality, concluding with, "She was one of a kind. I'll miss her." *And I'll keep my promise to help her, even though I failed while she was alive.*

"Anyone else wish to speak?" Doreen inquired.

The elderly aunt shifted in her wheelchair. "Speaking of difficult personalities, she had nothing on my brother. Winston made his first wife miserable, and after Cynthia died, I figured it was better if he stayed single."

"That's honesty for you," Tory whispered.

"To my astonishment, he and Malerie got along like a house on fire," the woman said. "Maybe it's because they were able to have children, which Cynthia couldn't. But also she stood up for herself. It was good for him."

"Thank you, Aunt Eunice," Danielle said.

"Let's pray." Into the silence, Fred intoned the twenty-third Psalm. The daylight dimmed when he reached the line, "Yea, though I walk through the valley of the shadow of death..."

A few people peered about as if expecting a ghostly apparition. However, it seemed to me some personalities are so forceful that a spectral presence would be overkill.

When the psalm ended, Doreen and Danielle hugged each other tearfully. They'd grown up in a family of five, of whom only two remained. Who had ripped their mother and sister from them?

Chairs squeaked against the tile floor. Fred reclaimed his wife and Heather stroked a strand of red hair from Doreen's cheek. The guests took their leave.

Soon only the sisters, their partners, Sandy, Tory and I remained. "As long as we're here, what can we do for your investigation?" Doreen asked.

"I'd like a copy of your mother's will and financial records," Tory said.

"So would I," said her client.

Fred seized the chance to challenge Heather. "Since you were her estate attorney, I presume you'll enlighten us."

"Client information is privileged."

"She's dead and these are her daughters. What are you hiding?"

Heather's face puckered as if she fought an internal battle. Finally, she said, "Mrs. Abernathy didn't change her will."

"Why not?" Fred demanded.

"She wasn't interested in setting up a trust, which I recommended, and she decided her existing will was adequate."

"Why did she consult you, then?"

Judging by her closed-in expression, Heather would prefer to remain silent. However, after a whispered word from Doreen, she said, "Her concern was whether Rafe Tibbets would inherit his wife's share of her estate. As for the terms of the old will, she said she'd left the money to her daughters, with no provisions for surviving spouses. I told her that, in my opinion, under California law, unless she had designated her son-in-law as an heir, he wouldn't benefit."

"You didn't see the will?" Tory probed. "Surely she brought it with her."

Heather's hands flew up in protest. "She claimed she couldn't find it. It had been drawn up soon after her husband died and she'd forgotten where she put it. Possibly with the papers she gave Dee Marie."

"Rafe was the attorney, right?" Doreen said. "He must have a copy."

"I recommended she request a printout for me to read. At a minimum, she needed an original signed copy in her possession. But that was the last I heard from her."

"When did this conversation take place?" Tory asked.

"About three months ago."

"I've never seen a will, old or new," Danielle said. "Doreen?"

"Me, either. Maybe it was stolen with the rest of the papers at Dee Marie's house, or else the police took it." She frowned. "I don't recall a will being listed on the property receipt."

"Property receipt?" Fred boomed. "Why haven't we seen that?"

"I'll send you a copy." Doreen shivered. "Honestly, it's creepy reading a list of Mom's stuff."

"I don't even know how much money she had, or where she invested it." Danielle halted the flow of words. "I shouldn't be thinking about that now."

"Why not?" her husband countered. "Don't get me wrong. Your mother and I may have crossed swords, but I mean no disrespect to her."

"Touching," Heather muttered.

Fred's nostrils flared. "My wife is entitled to her half of the estate. The sooner we sort this out, the sooner we can get on with having a baby."

Her half. Everyone assumed there were only the pair of them, but if a quadruplet existed, she, too, might stand to inherit. Of course, in order to stake a claim, the quad would have to step forward.

Why was I wasting mental energy on this preposterous idea? There was no quadruplet. Yet if Malerie hadn't planned to discuss her will, why *had* she insisted on seeing her daughters Friday evening?

"Regarding Mrs. Abernathy's estate, there's another matter that concerns me," Heather said.

"Don't keep us in suspense." Fred's words dripped sarcasm.

"As to whom she'd appointed executor, she believed it was her daughters," Heather explained. "But we can't be certain it wasn't Rafe."

"Why would she choose him?" Tory asked.

"When he drew up the will, Dee Marie was alive. He was both Malerie's son-in-law and her lawyer," Heather said. "She could have named him as a practical matter."

Doreen grimaced. "How much control would he have?"

"The executor tracks all assets, income and expenses during probate and files an accounting with the court," Heather said. "It would be his duty to distribute assets to the heirs and carry out terms of the will, such as special bequests."

Danielle reached for one of the remaining hors d'oeuvres, which Sandy was consolidating. "Could he take off with the money?"

"If he did, he'd be committing a crime. However, the law does grant an executor a percentage as payment."

"A percentage?" Fred repeated. "How much?"

"It depends on the value of the estate." Faced with a curious audience, Heather elaborated. "For a five million-dollar estate, I'd estimate his fee at about fifty thousand dollars."

Fred whistled. Danielle's eyes widened. "In other words, he earns a fat profit from Mom's death."

"There's a motive for murder," her sister said.

"For your mother, perhaps, but not for Dee Marie," Fred protested. "He'd have inherited far more if she'd survived. Besides, I'm convinced Rafe loved her."

"Men always swear they love their wives after they murder them," Heather said.

"And you think *I'm* biased?" Fred huffed.

Doreen broke in. "Rafe has a short fuse. I can't prove he ever hit my sister, but she missed more than one family gathering because of so-called illness."

I found this line of speculation disturbing. "She did suffer from asthma attacks." Also, as her doctor, I should have observed signs of abuse.

"Well, Rafe's the top suspect on my list," Danielle declared.

"I hear he refuses to talk to the police," Doreen added. "I'd like to throttle that smug bastard."

"I'm glad you think so highly of me." The raspy voice rang out from the entryway, where a departing guest must have left the door ajar.

Like an electric current, the words rippled through the small knot in the atrium. Normally, there was nothing imposing about Rafe Tibbets, who stood about five-foot-eight. This afternoon, though, anger twisted his narrow face and flashed in his pale eyes.

Mostly, what held us all motionless was the gun gripped in his hand.

CHAPTER EIGHT

My heart rate kicked up, my breath came fast and my blood pressure soared. Too bad my brain wasn't also ramping into high gear. We were seven people to one, which ought to provide options, yet I had zero notion what to do.

"Put the gun down," Tory barked. "Set it on the floor and move away." From her commanding tone, she might have been armed with a semi-automatic pistol and backed by a SWAT team.

Sandy, who'd been quietly collecting plates and cups, stood clutching a tray. I got the impression she was contemplating throwing it at Rafe.

The angular man kept the gun pointed at the floor. "I have a permit."

"I'll have to see that, please," Tory said.

"Why? Who the hell are you?"

Apparently remembering that she no longer had authority, she spread her hands placatingly. "I'm Tory Golden, a private investigator. I spoke to you on the phone. And even if you have a permit, it doesn't give you the right to brandish a firearm. Put it down or I'll be forced to make a citizen's arrest."

A couple of seconds trudged by before the man stuck the

weapon in a holster beneath his sport coat. "Don't get your panties in a twist. The safety was on."

Adrenaline continued pumping through my system. What guarantee did we have that he wouldn't draw the gun again? Or that he *had* engaged the safety? Or that safeties actually existed? My acquaintance with firearms was on a par with my experience of killers: until now, nil.

"If any of these people suffered a stress-induced heart attack, you could be charged with homicide." When his lip curled, Tory clarified, "Just advising you, sir."

"I had a right to draw a weapon. I feared for my life." In the months since he and Dee Marie visited my office, gray had invaded Rafe's brown hair and his shoulders seemed narrower, I registered when I'd calmed enough to see straight.

"We don't pose any danger to you," Doreen snapped.

"Then why were you threatening to strangle me?"

"That was hyperbole," Heather said. "Why the hell are you here?"

"To perform my legal duty." Rafe opened a briefcase I hadn't observed before, because his gun had dominated my entire range of vision. "It's my job as executor to distribute copies of Malerie's will to her daughters. Unless she drew up a new one?"

"Not as far as we know," Doreen said.

He removed sheaves of stapled papers and handed them out. The top page bore the name of his law firm.

"Give Heather a copy, too," Doreen said. "She's our probate attorney."

Fred's mouth opened as if to protest, but whatever he'd meant to say, he swallowed it. Under the circumstances, he could hardly advocate for his gun-toting brother-in-law to serve in that capacity.

As I'd learned after my wife's death, a probate attorney,

while not required, can assist the executor in filing court and tax documents. Under ordinary circumstances, Rafe could easily have handled those duties himself, but if I'd been one of the heirs, I wouldn't have trusted him, either.

"I'd appreciate a copy as well," Tory said.

Without comment, Rafe took out sheaves for Heather and Tory. For a few minutes, there was no sound except the rustling of paper as everyone read through the document. Over Tory's shoulder, I skimmed the main points. Aside from a small bequest to the Oahu Lane Animal Shelter, Malerie had left her property equally to her daughters and named Rafe as executor.

"Do you have an original bearing Mrs. Abernathy's signature?" Heather asked. "The court will require that."

"At my office," he said. "My mother-in-law had one, also."

"It appears to be missing," I told him. "And if you don't mind my asking, was that gun-waving bit for show or did you truly fear for your life?"

"I did and I do. Well, not as much since you're here, Doc. I consider you a man of integrity." His fleeting smile reminded me of his sister's. Since I couldn't picture Rafe with tattoos and purple hair, however, the resemblance ended there. "Think about it. The police and Dee Marie's family consider me the main suspect. If I die, they could clear the case and let the real murderer off scot free."

"Who do you suspect?" I asked, genuinely curious. "And why?"

"I'm glad somebody around here cares about the facts." Rafe glanced toward the refreshment table. "Man, I'm parched."

Sandy poured a glass of lemonade, which he drank thirstily. The guy obviously enjoyed prolonging his place at center stage.

"Well?" Doreen pressed when he finished. "Who do you suspect?"

"Heather, of course." He clicked his briefcase shut.

Heather's nostrils flared. "You're a certifiable loony."

"And you're a slimy opportunist."

"Get out of my house!" Anger shimmered in waves off her tiny frame.

Rafe didn't flinch. "Have you told these folks we used to work at the same law firm? And that you did everything in your power to sabotage me?"

"You're the one who spread rumors about *me*!" Heather retorted. "And landed a promotion you didn't deserve, when I'd been there longer and worked harder."

Too bad a messy family situation had thrown these old enemies together, but their feud was obscuring the issues. "Mr. Tibbets, would you please state your reasons for accusing Ms. Blythe?" I asked.

"Yes, do," Doreen growled. "I'm sure we could all use a good laugh."

"Gladly." As Rafe gathered his thoughts, the corners of his lips pulled down and his eyes lost focus, classic signs of sadness. "Dee Marie hated it when Doreen moved in with you. Not from anti-gay prejudice, I assure you. She remembered the lies you told about me at the law firm. You claimed I cheated on my wife, which was total crap. You hurt her *and* me."

"All's fair in love and war." Heather ducked her head, shutting out the disgust on Fred's face and the shock on Danielle's. And the disapproval on Doreen's.

"*Is* all fair in love?" Rafe demanded. "Dee Marie said the minute you found out her sister was an heiress, you pressured her to get married. Is that true, Doreen?"

"She proposed to me." The woman wrapped her arms around herself. "I told her I wasn't ready."

"Falling in love is no crime," Heather said. "I really care about Doreen."

The object of this declaration didn't respond. Doreen must

have been hurt. People assume that lesbians are kinder to each other than men are to women, but it's not necessarily true.

"There's more," Rafe said. "When Dee Marie began sorting through her mother's records, she discovered some kind of secret. I heard her on the phone squabbling with Malerie over it. Was it about you, Heather? Did you have business dealings with Malerie?"

Dots of red stood out on the woman's pale cheeks. "You're grasping at straws."

Rafe forged on. "I believe my wife threatened to expose your true nature to her mother. Your lies about my supposed cheating. Your scheming to marry Doreen. Plus whatever she discovered in those papers."

Heather tugged on a lock of hair that had tumbled from her topknot. "I had no business dealings with Mrs. Abernathy until three months ago, long after your wife's death. I didn't have any reason to kill Dee Marie."

"Well, somebody did," Rafe ground out. "And it was a person she knew."

"Why do you say that?" Tory had been following this exchange with keen interest. She'd tapped her phone frequently, taking notes and, I suspected, sending them to Keith.

"The police found no signs of forced entry." Rafe's eyes glittered. "We never trusted anyone with keys, not even our cleaning crew. Dee Marie let the killer inside. It wasn't a stranger."

"Those aren't facts, they're speculation," Heather declared. "You're just trying to deflect blame. She could have left the door unlocked or a window wide open. Maybe she gave someone a key and didn't tell you. Unless, of course, you're the killer."

Rafe flexed his fingers as if tempted to slip them into his

holster. I had visions of this argument deteriorating into a blood bath until Tory interjected, "I'm curious how you obtained a carry permit."

To score a concealed weapons permit from the Orange County sheriff, the applicant must show good cause. Although I've met a few physicians who carried guns legally after being threatened by disturbed patients, doctors are trained to preserve lives, not take them, and I'd never been tempted to apply. If your instincts and training aren't spot-on, the gun is more likely to be used against you than to stop an attack.

"I've received threats," Rafe said.

"Dissatisfied customers?" Heather taunted.

"When people are disinherited, they tend to vent their anger at the attorney. I'm sure you've experienced that."

"I've never felt it necessary to strut around with a pistol," was the response. "Well, you did your duty. Now get out."

Resentment flashed across his narrow face. However, this was her condo. "See you later, Ms. Probate Attorney." To Doreen and Danielle, Rafe said, "Despite what you may think, I loved your sister and I appreciated your mother's faith in me to execute her will."

"She'd forgotten she named you," Heather muttered.

"Had she really? Oh, one more item." Rafe paused dramatically before finishing, "When the police release her house, I need to go through it with you to list the valuables."

"Like hell," Doreen said. "That's an invasion of our privacy."

"The probate judge will require a full report."

"It does make sense," Tory pointed out.

"Leave your gun at home," Heather said. "This isn't the Wild West."

With a shrug, Rafe took his leave. Once the door closed, Fred regarded Tory. "Since you're supposed to be the expert, when will the police let us into the house?"

Although his tone must have grated, she replied evenly, "I expect within a day or so."

"I didn't ask what you expected, I asked when!" Danielle's husband seemed determined to vent at someone, and he'd chosen Tory.

"I'm curious how Rafe learned we were meeting here today," Danielle said coolly.

Good question. I supposed Morris could have overheard and mentioned it to Billie, but my father-in-law tends to be discreet.

Fred spoke up. "I called him so he could pay his respects. I didn't figure on him playing cowboy."

"You had no right!" Heather flared.

"Speaking of rights, I don't recall agreeing to hire you as the probate attorney." Fred scowled at the women around him. Over six feet tall and roughly two hundred and fifty pounds, he loomed large.

"You aren't an heir, so it isn't up to you." Doreen said.

"I'm protecting Danielle."

"My sister can speak for herself."

"You're the one trying to speak for her." Fred's puffy jowls took on a personality of their own. "And we don't appreciate you hiring this bungling lady PI to stick her nose in our business."

The gratuitous insult irked me. In view of the antagonism already befouling the air, however, I held my peace. Barely.

"Let's all take a deep breath." Tory's words reminded me that police are trained to de-escalate conflicts, not that they're necessarily great at it in their personal lives.

Instead of cooling off, Fred lashed out. "Why don't you shut up and stay out of it, bitch?"

There was a collective gasp from the women, as if he'd attacked each of them. In a sense, he had.

I'd heard enough. "Back off, Fred. You want to blame someone, blame me. I recommended Tory for this job because she's a hell of a good PI. And you should show more respect for women."

Too many emotions flew across his face for me to identify. His fists clenched, and there was a moment of suspended animation before he relaxed them. I guess he drew the line at punching out his wife's fertility doctor.

Once again, he directed his rage at Tory. "As for that interview we agreed to, it's canceled. You want information, get it from your damn client."

I have only a sketchy impression of the next few minutes: Danielle exchanging worried glances with her sister, Fred snarling at his wife until she accompanied him outside, and Sandy, aided by a subdued Heather, whisking away the refreshments. Oh, and Tory ignoring me while assuring Doreen she could still accomplish her job.

Inside her car, Tory gripped the steering wheel as if to rip it from the dashboard. "What the hell did you think you were doing?"

"Defending you." And the others, I nearly added, but I was in enough trouble already. Okay, they weren't powerless damsels, but I was raised to believe men should protect the women in our lives.

"For your information, I can defend myself. Don't do that again!"

"Wasn't planning to." I hoped that ended the conversation.

Switching on the ignition, Tory put the car in gear. We were halfway home before she burst out, "I was prepared for the Neanderthals at the P.D. to disrespect me, but you?"

"I respect you." Yet I had to admit that, under similar circumstances, I wouldn't have leaped to Keith's defense.

"Doreen and her husband are important witnesses, and I

don't appreciate you screwing that up." At a stop sign, she hit the brakes hard, jolting us forward.

"That's no reason to get us killed."

"Don't be ridiculous."

"I'm the one who landed this client for you," I noted. "Doesn't that show respect?"

"From now on, when it comes to my career, stay out of it."

"No problem." To accuse her of acting irrational would be pouring gasoline on the fire.

We rode the rest of the way home without a word. It bothered me, arguing with my sister-in-law, and I vowed not to let it result in an open breach. She was part of Lydia's family and had figured into my life since high school. Not to mention that, for the present, we occupied the same house.

I should have expected a blow-up eventually. She'd always had a fiery personality, although I disagreed with Lydia's assessment of Tory as a drama queen. Her freshman year, a junior had mocked her wild movements at a dance until a sharp kick to the knee sent him sprawling. She'd escaped punishment by claiming it was an accident, but for the rest of the year, guys had steered clear of her.

She hadn't yet popped me in the kneecap. But much as I might wish this quarrel was over, I suspected it wasn't.

CHAPTER NINE

It was a rough night. Despite the size of the house, my suite lies directly above the kitchen, and the floor shakes when someone slams the cabinets or the refrigerator. It's especially noticeable at midnight and again at 2 a.m.

Obviously, it was a restless night for Tory, too.

Although I don't schedule surgeries on Mondays, I'm in the habit of rising early and working out. Lydia and I equipped the retreat adjacent to the master bedroom with mats, a treadmill, an elliptical trainer and a bench for lifting weights.

Barely had I pulled on my exercise clothes before thumping noises alerted me that Tory had invaded the gym. Damn, why hadn't I listed it as off-limits when I was inventing rules?

Sharing the space had never been a problem with my wife. Unlike her sister, Lydia didn't grunt noisily and pound on the equipment. And she didn't toss glares in my direction when I entered.

Cutting my losses, I went for a run. Early mornings are lovely near the ocean, with mist softening the edges of the world.

That day, though, I barely noticed the springiness of my running shoes on the sidewalk or the hibiscus blooming in a neighbor's yard. I was too busy contemplating ways to keep Tory out of the exercise room. Buy a Keep Out sign? Install a lock? Or simply restrict her hours?

By the time I returned, she'd vanished, but the day's irritations were far from over. In the hospital parking garage, I found both lower-level charging slots in use. One of the cars I recognized as belonging to a pediatrician. The other was an exact match for mine, down to the color.

How had Jeremiah laid his hands on the car so fast, and didn't he care that that was *my* slot? Well, unofficially.

After finding a charging station on the next level, I headed in to see patients. Mondays are stressful, although not the busiest days in a doctor's office—Tuesdays hold that honor, I have no idea why, and Friday afternoons occasionally produce a pileup worse than on the freeways. Nevertheless, at the start of the week, the staff has to juggle patients anxious for a last-minute appointment, coupled with those who wait until they're already late before calling to cancel. Or who simply don't show up.

Weekends ought to produce relaxed, happy patients and personnel. Instead, the grouchiness factor goes off the charts. Mine included.

By lunch, I was in no mood for a snack from the break-room vending machine. While I rarely visited the hospital cafeteria and questioned the nutritional value of its gravy-laden specials, some days a guy deserves comfort food. Also, I learned during my residency that the rules of nutrition don't apply to doctors.

The day's special was meat loaf and mashed potatoes, with cooked carrots and yellow squash. "Healthy stuff," was the mocking verdict from the fellow behind me in line. Sporting a tie-dyed surgical cap, anesthesiologist Rod Vintner arched his eyebrows for effect. "That would be our mental health, of course."

"I'll do penance with a salad tonight."

Beyond the serving line, the large room rang with chatter from crowded tables. "They've got heat lamps on the patio," Rod observed after we paid for our meals.

"Sounds promising." I'm not sure why the doctors tend to congregate at the outdoor tables; probably for a break from the noise. When we stepped outside, I was pleased not to spot Jeremiah at either of the populated tables.

Rather than squeeze in, Rod and I chose an empty one. As he'd observed, the heat lamps took the edge off the cool air. A screen of flowering bushes provided privacy.

I prepared for a barrage of jokes. Rod had the biggest store of doctor humor I've ever encountered, along with a huge stock of lawyer barbs. In his early forties, he'd recently remarried and gained custody of his two preteen daughters after a wallet-busting battle.

"You may wonder why I singled you out today," he said.

I braced for the punch line.

"I understand Dr. Abernathy's widow was a patient of yours."

That didn't strike me as the opening for a gag. Unsure what to expect, I said, "True."

"And you're a friend of the homicide detective."

I didn't bother to ask how he knew that. In addition to collecting jokes, Rod's a gossip magnet. Even if he didn't snoop, anesthesiologists hear plenty of ear-bending conversations in the operating room.

"Right." And his point was...?

"I volunteer at the animal shelter, like Malerie. We're old acquaintances." Her late husband had been a colleague of Rod's, after all. "This may be neither here nor there, but she was always urging me to invest in the latest scheme. If you could believe her, every startup was the next Microsoft."

"Did you follow her advice?" I asked.

"No. I'm not much of a gambler," Rod said. "Just thought you might want to pass that along, in case it's helpful."

Everyone presumed Malerie had money, but maybe she'd become richer than they suspected. Or else she'd suffered losses. I hoped they weren't large, for her daughters' sakes. "Did her investments pay off?"

"I never heard." He glanced past me. "Uh oh. Here comes Dr. Weird."

I didn't have to ask who that was. "Maybe he'll join the others." *Yeah, right.*

"He's bee-lining in our direction," Rod said.

I considered diving behind an azalea bush. Too late.

"Eric! Rod!" Plopping a tray on our table, Jeremiah beamed at our plates. "We all bought the special."

"Amazing," Rod said.

Might as well satisfy my curiosity, I decided as the newcomer folded his rangy frame into a chair. "How did you get your new car so fast?" To Rod, I explained, "It's identical to mine. He just ordered it a few days ago."

"It arrived for another customer who changed his mind about the color," Jeremiah said. "I had told the dealer my order was urgent, so he called me."

"Why was it urgent?" Rod asked.

Surprise animated our companion's bony face. "Because I was driving around in a car like Eric's old one. What kind of impression does that give?"

Rarely have I seen Rod speechless. I had no comment, either.

With our conversation exhausted, the food disappeared rapidly. Doctors get in the habit of eating fast if we want to eat at all.

A topic occurred to me. "Is your new nurse working out?"

"I have not decided." Jeremiah gripped his water bottle. "Frankly, I could use your advice."

This was supposed to be the nurse's first day. How bad could she be? "Was she late?"

"Early," he said.

"Mix up the patients?"

"Certainly not."

Since we appeared to be playing twenty questions, Rod joined in. "Wear a Winnie-the-Pooh costume with feet in it?"

Jeremiah answered thoughtfully. "Why would she do that?"

"Ignore Rod," I said. "What's wrong with her?"

"She had a fight with her mother."

Not high on my list of reasons to reject an employee. "Right in the office?"

"On the phone," he said. "It lasted three minutes and twenty seconds before she rang off. Do you think I should fire her?"

"Seriously?" Rod asked.

"Personal problems do not belong in a doctor's office," Jeremiah replied. "And imagine, a grown woman arguing with her mother."

"If you ask me, it would be a rare woman who *doesn't* argue with her mother," Rod said.

Jeremiah kept his attention on me. "Well?"

Not only was a qualified nurse about to get the boot for acting human, but my fellow OB/GYN would then resume making life miserable for temps. "I would never cast off an employee over a minor kerfuffle," I said.

"A minor kerfuffle." Jeremiah mouthed the words appreciatively.

"Why not have your office manager suggest she confine personal calls to breaks?"

"Excellent counsel, Eric."

Afterwards, the term "a minor kerfuffle" buzzed in my head.

En route to my office, I realized why.

I'd been furious with my sister-in-law this morning over a minor matter. We should both apologize. Or let the matter ride. Either way, put it behind us.

She had a hot temper and I had a tendency to view her as Lydia's annoying kid sister. Old patterns were overdue to be laid to rest.

My thoughts returned to Malerie's impulsive investment strategy. While that bore checking out, I still lacked a clear picture of why a killer might have targeted her.

Greed over an inheritance? A dangerous old secret, or a more recent one? Like most of us, she hadn't led a blameless existence, especially if she'd once had an extramarital affair, but that was decades ago. And why had Dee Marie been killed?

The logical conclusion was that the stolen papers contained information that might harm the killer, but how? Did Malerie's investments open a window into a criminal conspiracy? As for my missing file, how could old medical data shed light on the situation?

That brought me back to her far-fetched claim about a quadruplet, which implied that my father, Isaiah and their staff had conspired to steal a baby. Why? To sell it on the black market? Nonsense.

A busy afternoon kept my thoughts occupied with patients. It was nearly six when I arrived home, where the sight of an unfamiliar brown compact at the curb reminded me that our new cleaning lady had started work.

My plan of dining on a salad vanished the moment I stepped inside. The dominant aromas, beyond the lemony scent of furniture cleaner, were balsamic vinegar and garlic.

This house used to be a refuge for my father and me, and later for Lydia, its many rooms allowing each our privacy. Today, the bustle of activity, although centered in the kitchen, filled every nook and transformed every molecule of air.

I expected a spurt of annoyance. Instead, my stomach rumbled happily. I had no desire to pitch these people out.

At the stove, Morris stirred zucchini slices and balsamic vinegar in a large frying pan. An aproned Sandy, a scarf over her blond hair, was setting out utensils, napkins and paper plates.

"Wouldn't you rather use that beautiful china?" she asked. "It's a shame to leave it in the cabinet."

"Too much cleanup." At the free-standing counter that divided the kitchen from the great room, Tory was hacking a watermelon into chunks.

"Where's Billie?" I'd been concerned about the delivery woman after her traumatic discovery.

Morris switched off the burner. "She felt well enough to make deliveries again. I invited Sandy to join us for dinner."

The housekeeper smiled, light-green eyes lively in her square face. "Good to see you again, Dr. Darcy."

"Glad you're here."

"She's a whirlwind," Morris told me. "The house is spotless."

"I hope you're not in a hurry to return to Iowa," I said.

Whack! went Tory's butcher knife. "Idaho."

"Right."

"Why would she want to leave?" Tory prodded.

I directed my answer to Sandy. "You moved here to support Malerie, right? I thought you might have family in Idaho."

"Not any more. Both my parents are gone." She filled water glasses from a pitcher. "Boise's beautiful. Its name comes from the French word for trees, and it lives up to that. But I prefer the weather in Southern California."

"Why did you leave Safe Harbor in the first place?" I noticed the rice cooker's display indicated it had five minutes left.

"Family reasons," Tory filled in. Clearly, she'd questioned

the witness earlier. "And she quarreled with Malerie about her affair with Dr. Abernathy."

"I'm no prude but I draw the line at adultery." Sandy waved a dismissive hand. "That was ages ago."

"It's quite a story," Morris put in. "People sneaking around the hospital having affairs, like on *Grey's Anatomy*."

"Also, the timing worked out for me to leave California, since my family needed me." Sandy set tongs in the salad bowl. "Malerie and I stayed in touch. Even though we disagreed about her choices, we were friends."

"So you followed the events over the next few years." I glanced at Tory for confirmation. She kept her gaze on the watermelon.

"It devastated her when Winston broke it off." Sandy shook a carafe of salad dressing. "But she respected his attempt to save his marriage. Well, accepted might be a better word."

"They reconnected when he was in the hospital," Morris said eagerly. "Love bloomed all over again."

I'd heard about this before. "His wife had died in the car crash, right? Anything suspicious about it?"

"Of course not!" Sandy regarded me indignantly.

"I didn't mean to insult Mrs. Abernathy," I qualified.

"A drunk driver T-boned their car," Tory told the air. "He was convicted of manslaughter."

"You've done your research," I said.

"It's called investigating."

"That was a compliment," I growled. "Never mind."

Morris's hands traced nervous arcs. Any hostility in the family upset him. "I forgot to toast walnuts to serve on the side," he said. "I'll get them." He ducked into the pantry.

"He has clients with allergies to tree nuts as well as peanuts," Tory told Sandy. "Even at home, if the recipe lists nuts, he leaves them out."

"I'm glad he's careful," the housekeeper said. "I understand Malerie's son-in-law nearly died once from—what's it called?"

"Anaphylactic shock," I said. "I'm sure Rafe keeps an EpiPen at hand." The devices provide a quick injection of epinephrine, which restores breathing, blood pressure and other vital functions.

The doorbell chimed. "Must be Keith. His stomach clock is infallible." Tory jumped up, nearly overturning the bowl in front of her. "I'll get it."

She'd rather face her ex-boyfriend than hang around me. Well, in view of her touchiness, that suited me too. Also, being alone with the housekeeper allowed me to pose a delicate question. "Sandy, do you recall anything strange about the triplets' birth?"

"Isn't the birth of triplets unusual enough?" She set the fruit on the table

"I mean, other than that. A detail Malerie might have mentioned?" I didn't want to influence her testimony by bringing up the quad theory.

"Not really."

"How did she react when the girls were born? Was she depressed?" If I followed the chronology correctly, there'd been a two-year gap between Malerie and Winston's split and their subsequent marriage, and another two years before the triplets' birth. Sandy would have been in Idaho that whole period.

"Just the opposite." She sponged watermelon juice and rind off the counter. "She and Dr. Abernathy were thrilled. He and Cynthia couldn't have children. Three kids in one pregnancy struck Malerie as a sign from heaven."

"Producing triplets indicated God's forgiveness for adultery?" I mused.

Returning from the pantry, Morris tossed nuts into the

frying pan and set them to sizzling. "That seems more like superstition than religion."

"That's true of a lot of what passes for religion these days, isn't it?" Sandy said.

As we spoke, I tracked noises from the front: the door opening, low voices, footsteps, then Keith's ring tone, followed by, "Detective Sparks... Yes?"

Tory rounded the corner. "I was right; it's Keith. He'll just be a minute."

Morris slid the toasted walnuts onto a saucer. While everyone else dawdled, I filled my plate with the savory zucchini dish, rice and nuts. Feeling like a kid sneaking cookies—or a medical resident refueling—I began to eat.

Keith's voice grew louder as he approached. "When? Where? I'd appreciate that. Thanks for the tip, fre...friend."

My brain filled in the name of the tipster: Fred.

As soon as I saw Keith's face, I knew something big was happening. And that I might have to leap into action.

I ate faster.

CHAPTER TEN

"Tory, call your client." Keith's tone was grim.

She took out her cell. "What's up?"

"Rafe Tibbets has summoned the family to an emergency meeting," Keith said. "No reason provided, and no police allowed."

"Can he do that?" Morris asked.

"Yes. He's the executor of the will and it's a private matter." Keith was twitching with frustration. "Tory, ask Doreen if you and Eric can attend. I need details of everything that's discussed, including how each person reacts to whatever bombshell he drops."

"You got it." She swung into action as if they were a team.

While they sorted out the details, my cast-iron stomach absorbed multiple mouthfuls of food. Wish I'd been able to taste more of it.

Sandy offered to join us as an extra set of eyes and ears. We declined, however, since Doreen was probably pushing her luck by inviting Tory and me. Too many people and Rafe might throw us all out.

Tory insisted on driving separately from me. She had to be free to go wherever the case took her afterwards, she explained tersely.

"I was hoping we could talk," I said when we reached the hall, away from the others.

Her chin thrust out, pointy enough to poke holes in an apology. "Don't worry, I'll stay the hell out of your man cave from now on."

"That wasn't what I wanted to discuss." I'd have liked to clear the air, and riding together would provide an opportunity.

"I have work to do."

"Understood." I respected her dedication. Wasn't sure what I'd have said, anyway, since I didn't believe I was in the wrong for trying to protect her.

With his taste for drama, Rafe had summoned the clan to Malerie's house, which the police had released that afternoon. Gone were the flashing emergency vehicles, the crime-scene tape and the crowd of neighbors from four days ago. Only a porch light penetrated the evening gloom, casting a glow across the stone facing and steeply slanted eaves.

Despite the pretty setting, dread closed over me. Why had Rafe commanded our presence? Maybe he'd stumbled across a dark secret that I should have guessed in time to save Malerie.

Tory and I pulled up a few seconds apart. Doreen, who'd been watching, met us at the curb.

"Whatever game Rafe's playing, I value you both as witnesses." She wore her nurse's uniform and Heights View Medical Center ID. She must have driven straight from the hospital.

"We should apprise Detective Sparks of anything we learn," Tory said.

"I'm counting on it."

Heather clicked up to join us. She hadn't changed since work either, I gathered from her tailored suit and those high heels adding inches to her small frame.

"I don't trust him," she said. "I suppose that's a given."

"No one trusts him." Doreen slipped her arm around Heather's shoulders. Whatever their differences, they hadn't become estranged.

Inside, Danielle greeted us with, "Oh, good, you're all here."

A tiled entryway overlooked the sunken living room. Malerie's taste ran to gold-flocked wallpaper, brocade curtains and dark wood cabinets displaying vases and figurines. In a few places, traces of fingerprint powder lingered, as did a hint of cigarette smoke. Unless it had survived for years, she'd continued smoking despite doctor's orders.

Well, under the circumstances, she no longer risked cancer, stroke or emphysema.

The thin man pacing in front of the fireplace cocked an eyebrow at me but didn't comment. There was no bulge under Rafe's jacket as far as I could tell.

Behind him on the mantel, a photo showed the teenage triplets laughing, red hair blending into a swirl. More framed shots: Malerie with Winston Abernathy, his face wreathed in happy wrinkles; Malerie with her girls, about age five; Danielle and Fred in a wedding pose; Dee Marie alone in a white gown; Doreen in her nurse's uniform. No Rafe, and, not surprisingly, no Heather.

Family members settled around the room. Fred occupied a recliner that accommodated his bulk, with Danielle perched on the arm. Heather and Doreen sat side by side on the flowered couch. Tory and I remained standing on the tile.

To our right, I had a partial view of the kitchen with its checkered wallpaper and shelves of country-style ceramic ware. Past French doors lay the pool area where Malerie had breathed her last.

I couldn't shake the sense that she was depending on me.

That, as I'd told Keith, she'd handed me a key.

Rafe cleared his throat. "Let's do this." Grim determination replaced his previous air of bravado. "As executor, it's my job to track the deceased's assets. Although my access is limited until I have a death certificate, I've started preliminary inquiries. Because you all mistrust me, and to avoid any appearance of secrecy, I mean to keep you fully informed."

"Get to the point," Fred grumped. I'd have bet he, too, had been dragged from his meal.

"Today, I contacted Malerie's stockbroker, bank manager and insurance agent," Rafe said. "The bottom line is that your mother appears to have been pretty close to broke when she died."

A stunned pause reflected our shock. I'd assumed the estate was worth as much as a million dollars.

Follow the money. If we did, where would it lead?

"That's impossible." Doreen leaned forward. "Dad left her well provided for."

"I'm aware of that." For a change, Rafe didn't appear to relish his position at center stage. "But he died four years ago."

"Money doesn't simply vanish. Where did it go?" Fred demanded.

Rafe studied a paper in his hands. "According to her stockbroker, Malerie insisted on placing investments against his advice. I'm trying to determine what influenced her choices."

That matched what Rod Vintner had told me, except that things had been worse than I'd imagined. Tory, meanwhile, was taking rapid notes on her phone, presumably forwarding them to Keith.

"Have you looked into this stockbroker?" she asked.

"He handled Winston's account for decades. But I'll keep that in mind."

So, I presumed, would Tory and Keith.

"Hold on," Danielle said. "Even if Mom lost her savings, my parents each had a quarter-million dollar life insurance policy. Dad insisted on it."

"According to her agent, she had a twenty-year policy that matured last year," Rafe said. "Since she was turning sixty and faced a hip replacement, the insurance company jacked up the premium. She decided not to renew."

"She can't have lost it all." Heather squeezed Doreen's hand. "I mean, she wouldn't be that foolish."

"There's a small amount left in mutual funds," Rafe said. "Plus a few thousand in savings and checking accounts. I can't find any record of a safe deposit box, but I'll keep searching in case she did business at a second bank. With most of her documents missing, it's hard to tell."

What a cascade of disasters. "Mrs. Abernathy owned this house, didn't she?" I said. "It has to be worth a substantial amount."

"When the cash ran short, she took out a reverse mortgage," Rafe said. "That provided a lump sum. Properly invested, it should have produced an adequate monthly income."

Fred's eyelids lowered as if he were about to dive into icy waters. "Don't tell me she gambled that away, too."

"She invested it with her usual creativity."

"Who the hell was advising her?" Doreen snarled. "Whoever it was, they killed her to cover their tracks, didn't they?"

"The stockbroker claims not to know," Rafe said. "Maybe she was following Internet tips."

"From who?" Fred pressed.

"I'll do my best to find out."

"That could be what Dee Marie stumbled across." Tears dampened Danielle's lashes. "And it got her killed."

As far as I knew, Internet fraudsters plied their scams from afar. Whoever had killed mother and daughter had done it up close. To me, that implied the source of those recommendations had been nearer home. But I was here to observe, not spin theories.

"Won't the police look into Mom's finances?" Doreen asked.

Gazes shifted toward Tory. "That would be standard procedure in a murder case."

"Since they've been less than impressive in identifying my wife's killer, I prefer to do my own digging," Rafe said.

"I'm sure you will, or so you'd like us to believe." Heather's anger seemed to spring from nowhere, until I recalled that she and Rafe had a longstanding enmity. "After all, you conveniently had her papers and laptop disappear from your house. The one to which you and your late wife zealously guarded your keys."

"If the family doubts my word, they're welcome to talk directly to her broker and her banker. Here's their contact information." Rafe handed business cards to each of the daughters and to Tory. "And if we're to work together on the probate, Heather, I expect you to avoid leveling baseless accusations. Otherwise, that might raise questions about your motives."

"Stop it!" Danielle wailed. "Our mother isn't even buried and you're picking over her corpse."

"I'm sorry," Heather said.

"Speaking of burials," Doreen broke in. "I heard from the funeral home late today that her body's been released, so we can schedule the service. I sent you an email, Danielle."

Her sister poked at her phone. "Oh, here it is."

"Did she leave instructions about the service, or is it up to us to ensure things are done properly?" Fred asked. "People do still pray at funerals, I presume."

"The will states only that she's to be buried in a prepaid plot beside her husband," Rafe put in. "The details are up to the heirs."

"Good," Fred said. "I'll see if our pastor's available."

"The hell you will." Doreen shot off the couch.

Heather arose, too. "There's no way we'd let that homophobic, redneck minister spew his hate theology at Mrs. Abernathy's service."

"Danielle and I will never allow your left-wing, transsexual *thing* to deliver her eulogy!"

So much for hoping the conflict might subside.

"You heard Doreen." Unexpectedly, Danielle's voice cut through the rhetoric. "The decision is hers and mine. Not Heather's and not yours, Fred."

Her husband fell silent for a nanosecond, but only to catch his breath. "Whose side are you on?"

"Why do I have to be on anyone's side?"

Her response irked Fred. "Because you have a moral obligation to stand by your husband!" His voice shrilled to a high note that hurt my ears.

"You mean to knuckle under, don't you?" Heather threw in.

"Exactly what I'd expect from you, trying to undermine our marriage," Fred roared. "You lesbos don't have a clue what a real marriage is."

"If you're the prime example, God save us," Doreen said.

"How dare you take His name in vain?" He leveraged himself upright, towering over the pair. When Heather assumed a pugnacious stance, Fred's fists tightened.

Beside me, Tory braced to intervene. Shorter than Fred at five-foot-ten, she was in better condition and well trained. I was ready to provide assistance as well, although I doubted she'd appreciate it.

Rafe quelled them with a sneer. "You idiots slug it out if you insist. I'm more interested in the fact that hundreds of thousands of dollars have vanished. That means we finally have a motive for why someone killed my wife and her mother."

"Don't be ridiculous," Heather said. "The money might have nothing to do with it."

"For six months the police have turned my house upside down and invaded my privacy," Rafe snarled. "I'm sick of it. Whoever did this, I have a damn good idea how to track them down, and I'm not counting on the cops to do it for me."

With that declaration, he whipped out of the house. In the lingering chill, I wondered whether it occurred to him that if the killer was in this room, he or she had just heard the threat. And might act on it.

CHAPTER ELEVEN

Since no one was in the mood to stick around, Tory and I left. "You've been texting Keith?" I asked on the way to our cars.

She nodded. "I'll fill him in on the rest while I drive." On her hands-free phone, I presumed.

I switched to another matter that bothered me. "I'm concerned about Danielle. She has to go home with Fred and he's a loose cannon."

"She doesn't *have* to go home with him. She's an adult." Tory halted at her sedan, directly in front of Ada's house.

"Relationships are complicated," I said. "And I feel responsible for her."

"Why, because she's your patient?" Beneath a streetlamp, Tory's face was shadowed. "You must have the world's most massive ego to think you're in charge of everyone who consults you. Get over yourself."

She stomped around to the driver's side. Exasperated, I drove home through sparsely traveled streets, taking a different route to avoid trailing Tory.

Her comment had been uncalled-for. To me, my role as a doctor extended beyond reaching a diagnosis and prescribing medication or surgery.

I've met a number of doctors who aim to save lives but find patients annoying. Some regard suffering as little more than a challenging presentation of symptoms. Although I hadn't been that insensitive, it was true that, as a medical student, I'd viewed each woman solely as she existed at that moment. Her medical history had been nothing more than that: history.

In practice, I'd learned to place each person on a continuum, transitioning through the stages of her life. While I couldn't swear I loved each of my patients, we established a bond of trust that, as long as they remained in my care, we would travel a path together.

Murder disrupted that journey. It didn't end my commitment. If that reflected a huge ego, so be it.

Unlike coastal communities that flaunt their clubs and cafés, Safe Harbor mostly goes dark at night. After I swung onto the main boulevard, the six lighted stories of the medical center rose like a beacon ahead on my right.

I lowered my window to enjoy the sea breeze. A few minutes later, when I entered my driveway, a cloud of perfume blew in from a jasmine bush Lydia had planted, a sadly sweet reminder that I couldn't save everyone.

In the kitchen, Tory leaned against the counter, shoveling down leftovers from a container. She'd missed dinner, and I wondered if hunger had sharpened her temper earlier.

"You should follow the doctor's diet." I opened the fridge.

"What's that, stuff your face when you get the chance?"

"Exactly." I retrieved a package of dates dusted with coconut. It never pays to miss dessert.

My brain searched for a neutral topic of conversation. Any reiteration of my worry for Danielle might land us right back in touchy territory.

Finally, I said, "An anesthesiologist who volunteers at the

animal shelter told me Malerie often passed along investment advice."

"Such as?"

"He didn't recall specifics."

She set the container aside. "What's his name?"

"Rod Vintner." I hadn't meant to imply that she ought to interview him. *Let her decide how to do her job.*

Tory jotted a note in her cell. "In case you're interested, I backgrounded the love fest between Heather and Rafe."

"Love fest" was typical ironic cop speak. Similar to junior high, when classmates labeled my skinny self "the Hulk" until, at the start of ninth grade, I showed up six inches taller and twenty pounds heavier, mostly muscles. A couple of girls started referring to me as "the Hunk," but, mercifully, that didn't stick, either.

"I'm interested." I took a seat at the counter.

Scanning her notes, Tory said, "Ada Humphreys—Malerie's neighbor— suggested I talk to her son, Geoffrey. He's a family attorney acquainted with both parties."

"I've heard of him." An associate from his office had presented a talk to the staff recently on laws affecting surrogacy and egg donations.

"The feud started when Rafe and his newly minted law license joined the Santa Ana firm where Heather worked. He got fast-tracked ahead of her. Sexism, anti-gay bias, or maybe it was a matter of competence. Hard to tell."

"Why'd they leave?" Both now ran their own offices.

"The firm's principals were accused of embezzling clients' funds," Tory said. "Attorneys administer trusts and lawsuit payouts, so they handle a lot of money. When the DA filed charges, the staff fled the sinking ship."

"Any chance the firm represented Malerie?"

"No obvious connection. Besides, that was well before her

husband died."

"So now Rafe and Heather are competing with each other for business," I summarized. "And for respect on the home front."

Tory tapped her fingers on the counter. She had more on her mind. Abruptly, she said, "Did you know?"

I'd been mulling whether to finish off the last three dates, and had just concluded that leaving so few would merely taunt the next hungry person. "Know what?"

"That Keith was cheating on me."

I forgot about eating. "Certainly not. I heard it from Morris after the fact."

"Keith's your best friend. Doesn't he tell you stuff?" At close range, gold flecks shone in her green eyes. Lydia's had been the dark brown of bitter chocolate.

"Guys don't do heart-to-hearts," I said. "I wasn't even aware you were in a relationship until you brought him to Morris's Seder last year."

Despite not being religious, my father-in-law celebrates food-related holidays such as Passover, where the story of the Israelites' suffering and escape from Egypt is retold at a ceremonial dinner. "Lydia and I were both stunned."

"You hid it well."

"In medical school, I got an A-minus in Remaining Impassive When Shocked."

"What was the minus for?"

"Babies with two heads," I deadpanned. As long as we were discussing her relationship—well, sort of—I indulged my curiosity. "Why did you move in with him right after Lydia died? The timing seemed odd." Although they'd been dating for months, until then she'd remained fiercely independent.

Tory wedged her container onto the dishwasher's top rack. "Do you remember—oh, of course you do."

"What?"

"How we broke the news about my sister."

"Indelibly." It had been early evening when the doorbell rang. I'd opened it to find Keith and Tory, both in uniform, Tory's face red from crying.

The Bureau of Consular Affairs had requested that the police notify the family of Lydia Darcy that she had died in Israel. In cases like this, it's best to send someone in person to provide support until relatives can arrive.

When word reached the department, Keith heard it first. He must have been shaken, but he'd gone to inform Tory and held her as she wept.

Once she got a grip on her emotions, she'd insisted on accompanying him to tell me. Later, I'd appreciated how hard that must have been for them. At the time, I'd felt like a wall of water had smashed into me, throwing me wrong side up in the surf until I couldn't breathe.

After months of estrangement from Lydia that I didn't understand, after fearing my wife had grown to hate me or had sunk into a profound depression, I couldn't begin to sort out my emotions. I'd gone numb.

Too stubborn to admit I was in shock, I'd brushed off their protests and sent them away. Moving stiffly up the stairs, I'd tripped and fallen. Thank goodness I'd had my phone with me or I might have lain there for hours. Still, I'd been too badly injured to travel and bury my wife.

Tory's voice restored me to the present. "After I went to Israel, Keith invited me to move in. My lease was up, and I couldn't stand the thought of living alone."

"And now?" I asked.

"What do you mean, now?"

Just when we were getting along, I hated to put my foot in it. But I'd sensed glimmers of hope for Keith. "You guys function well as a team. Any chance he could win you back?"

Her expression tightened. "Why, so he can go on proving I can't count on him? That when I need him, he might be too busy boffing another woman? No, we don't function well as a team anywhere outside work."

"Sorry," I said.

She eyed the remaining dates. "You planning to eat those?"

"All yours." With a twinge of regret, I pushed them over.

As she ate, I listened to familiar house noises: the hum of electronics, the rumble of the icemaker, Morris's faint snoring from the downstairs bedroom. And felt a jumble of emotions radiating from my sister-in-law.

Tory licked her fingers before saying, "I'm busy in the morning but I'll check on Danielle later. I'd prefer to interview her without her husband. She works at Kitchens, Cooks and Linens, right?"

"Yes."

"Oh, and Eric?"

I lifted an eyebrow.

"As soon as I can afford it, I'll rent my own place." Tory whisked off before I could comment.

I'd wanted her to move out, but not like this. At least we were still on speaking terms.

I trained my thoughts on tomorrow. While Tory pursued her inquiries, I planned to do some investigating, too.

*

At lunch, it proved impossible to divide Rod from the audience of doctors enjoying his jokes. I cornered him afterwards, only to learn he couldn't recall a single detail of Malerie's recommendations.

"How about anyone else Mrs. Abernathy might have shared tips with?" Surely she'd spread the word to others.

He provided the names of a few fellow volunteers. I texted

them to Tory and got a smiley face in return.

One more question for Rod: Had he observed peculiar behavior or signs of dementia in Malerie?

"To me, she seemed normal," he responded. "Chatty and careless with money, as if Winston had left her a bottomless pit of it. But no more than usual."

"Careless how?"

"Those investments, for one thing," Rod said. "Also, whenever the shelter had a fundraiser, they could rely on her to make up the difference so it reached its goal."

"Thanks." How odd, considering her reputation for stinginess. She must have had a fondness for vulnerable creatures. People were often contradictory, in my experience.

In midafternoon, a patient cancellation left me a spare half-hour. Retiring to my private office, I reviewed what we'd learned so far.

Item: Six months ago, someone had smothered Dee Marie and stolen her laptop, along with papers belonging to her mother. Police suspected her husband, but he had an alibi and no clear motive, unless he'd been bilking Malerie.

I pictured Rafe's narrow face. Quite a coincidence that his sister had discovered Malerie's body. The police must think so, too.

Back to the facts:

Item: Malerie had lost hundreds of thousands of dollars, maybe more when you factored in the value of her house. No indication where she'd obtained her misleading tips or who had profited, aside from the broker who claimed he'd carried out her directions against his better judgment.

Item: She'd commented to me that people lied, then invited her daughters to her house for an announcement. Whatever it was, it might have prompted the killer to take her life.

Item: She'd been heard arguing with an unidentified

woman shortly before her death.

Item: Malerie had consumed a large number of blood-pressure pills that presumably contributed to her drowning.

Item: It was possible that both victims had known their murderer or murderers. Dee Marie had allowed the person inside, and Malerie hadn't screamed for help, which her neighbor would likely have heard.

Speculation: There'd been a secret in the missing papers that someone considered worth killing for, possibly related to theft. He or she must have considered the subject closed after smothering Dee Marie, until learning that Malerie had become suspicious and summoned her surviving daughters.

But this might not have been about money at all. Item: Last week, Malerie had spotted a woman who resembled her daughters so strongly that, coupled with her vivid dreams, the sighting had convinced her she'd borne quadruplets. Her digitized medical record shed no light on the situation.

Item: My house had been burglarized and her more extensive paper file had vanished.

Since Farrah hadn't yet signaled the arrival of my next patient, I clicked to Malerie's records and read through the orthopedic surgeon's report about her hip replacement. He'd used a minimally invasive technique and, with the aid of physical therapy and an old friend's care, she'd recovered well.

Did Sandy know more than she'd revealed about Malerie's secrets? Although they'd stayed in touch, she'd left Safe Harbor prior to her friend's marriage, and had been living in Idaho when the triplets were born. She had mentioned disapproving of the extramarital affair, but aside from that, I'd sensed she was trying to be discreet.

Tempted as I was to grill her next week when she cleaned my house, that was hardly fair to an employee. Also, I admired her loyalty to Malerie. And my remaining questions might stem more from nosiness than from any relevance to the crimes.

I was curious as to why Winston had broken off his affair with Malerie. Had his first wife, Cynthia Abernathy, discovered he was cheating and threatened a divorce that might strip him of his assets? California being a community property state, that could have included half the value of his medical practice.

Had he or Malerie arranged Cynthia Abernathy's demise? The car crash had seriously injured Winston, and could have killed him. Also, according to Tory's research, a drunk driver had been convicted. Still, Malerie—and Winston, whose injuries might have been unintended—had benefited from Cynthia's death.

Was someone now seeking revenge? Did Cynthia have relatives who harbored a grudge? Surely Keith and Tory were pursuing this possibility.

Also, Tory had planned to interview Danielle today. A current of unease ran through me, that we'd left the young woman to deal with her husband's anger last night. While I'd seen no indications that Fred abused her mentally or physically, he might be a powder keg.

"You must have the world's most massive ego to think you're in charge of everyone who consults you." Tory hadn't been entirely wrong, I supposed.

My nurse appeared and informed me that a patient required my attention. For the rest of the afternoon, I had a full schedule, and didn't finish until nearly six p.m. I was descending via the stairs—for a little extra exercise—when my cell rang.

"Get over to the store fast. Fred's losing it." Tory broke off to snap, "You stay right there, buster. I don't care what your wife says, one more move and I'm calling the police."

In the background, I heard Danielle command, "An inch closer to those wine glasses and I'll call them myself."

How sad that she valued the glasses more than her safety. "Isn't there a manager who could intervene?" I asked.

"Danielle just got promoted to that position," Tory said. "Eric, we're in a holding pattern but I'm not sure how long it will last."

"On my way." I quickened my pace down the steps.

CHAPTER TWELVE

On the short drive, I reviewed what I knew of the Jeffers couple. They'd married six years ago, when she was twenty-one and Fred twenty-four. After I joined my father's practice and she became my patient, I'd noticed that she often deferred to her husband. However, she wasn't entirely submissive and he appeared to treat her with respect.

Their infertility stemmed from Danielle's history of severe pelvic inflammatory disease. She'd been sexually active in her teens with multiple partners and had suffered from chlamydia, which is curable with antibiotics. However, the infection hadn't initially caused symptoms and, before it was caught, her reproductive system suffered irreversible damage.

Later, she'd experienced a religious conversion and met Fred at a church singles group. Despite her past, which she'd disclosed, he'd fallen in love with her and they'd faced their medical issues as a couple.

Their relationship might be changing, though. Since Malerie's death, Fred had acted rigid, and last night's confrontation had indicated Danielle was no longer content to let her husband define their position on her family's matters. Was Fred flexible enough to share power, or was he primed to lash out?

Kitchens, Cooks and Linens was located on a side street. When I entered, the glass door activated soft chimes and an orange-spice fragrance floated in the air. Surrounded by dishes and glassware, I moved gingerly, half-convinced that my elbows could smash china at a dozen paces.

No one staffed the checkout counter. A convex mirror in a corner revealed a trio of tense figures in an area defined by free-standing bookshelves. A directional sign pointed to the Cookbook Nook.

Tory greeted me with a tilt of the head. Danielle, wearing a red-and-white checkered smock, continued addressing the man looming over her. "I don't see what there is left to say. According to your minister, I either bow down or you throw me out."

"He's *our* minister. And it's a matter of obedience to God, not to me or him." Despite an edge to his voice, Fred hung onto his self-control.

"That's according to Pastor Vald," Danielle responded. "And I resent your consulting him about *my* family."

"It's my family, too." Only a flick of Fred's eyes indicated he'd registered my arrival in their little group. "And why shouldn't I visit my spiritual leader?"

"I'm not sure I'd describe him as spiritual."

"We prayed together," Fred said. "We prayed for you."

"To kneel at your feet?"

Although the Cookbook Nook offered several canvas chairs, no one was sitting. I judged it wise to remain upright, too. As Tory had warned, there was no telling whether Fred might explode.

My sister-in-law remained balanced and ready for action. Even without a gun, Tory had plenty of defensive skills— offensive too, if necessary.

"You're mischaracterizing this." To me, Fred explained, "Last night my wife slept on the couch. This morning, she left without speaking to me. Since she refuses to join me in seeking counsel, I went alone. I don't suppose you're familiar with Pastor Vald?"

"Only by reputation." Pastor Vald had landed on the news when an established church ousted him in a dispute over his preaching on the role of women. After relocating his followers to a store-front, he'd launched a controversial blog and recorded a series of fiery sermons for YouTube.

While I wasn't qualified to assess his theology, I certainly didn't endorse his quasi-medieval views about marriage or God. As for my own religious convictions, I believed there *ought* to be a divine presence but, since Lydia's death, preferred not to think about it.

"Somebody has to remember what the Bible says and how God requires us to live," Fred said.

Tory started to roll her eyes, noticed my frown and schooled her features.

"Tell him the rest," Danielle demanded.

"There's no reason to repeat it."

"Yes, there is!" To me, she burst out, "Our so-called pastor harped on what a tramp I am. According to him, we're childless as a punishment. By refusing to let him preach at my mother's funeral, I'm proving once again that I'm an unfit wife."

"This isn't about the past," Fred huffed. "It's about respect for your husband. You're refusing to bend your will."

"I'm refusing to let that man pass judgment on my sister and Heather at our mother's funeral," Danielle retorted.

"Better than allowing Doreen to corrupt you!"

"Homosexuality isn't catching."

"That's not what I meant."

The chimes ushered in customers. After casting a stern look

at her husband, Danielle headed over and, apparently in response to a request, directed the young couple to the bath section.

Rejoining us, she picked up where she'd left off, in a more muted tone. "Doreen has as much right as I do to choose who officiates."

"You should have stood by me, even if we don't prevail," Fred snapped. "It was disloyal."

"Either I alienate my sister or you cast me off because I'm a slut?"

"That's unfair!"

"It's totally fair!"

They traded glares. Then they did something unexpected and unwelcome. In fact, terrifying.

They turned to me with hopeful expressions.

"Dr. Darcy," Fred said. "You understand us as well as anyone. How do we resolve this?"

The simplest response would have been to refer the pair to the hospital's psychologist, whose fertility group they attended. But since they were counting on me for suggestions, I decided to do my best.

"Let's start with common ground," I said. "You both want to save your marriage. Correct?"

Slowly, they nodded.

"Fred, did you truly forgive your wife for her youthful behavior?" That seemed a better term than "sins."

"Yes." He spoke emphatically.

"Was that forgiveness conditional?" I pressed. "Did she have to promise never to disagree with you? To accept you as her absolute authority?"

Shakily, as if asked to walk across hot coals, he said, "No."

Danielle peered toward the customers. They appeared to be busy picking out towels.

"So Danielle's respect for your..." *Choose carefully.* "...position as her husband doesn't require her to follow blindly?" I'd read once that courtroom attorneys never ask a question to which they don't already know the answer. Lucky that I'd gone into medicine instead of law, because I had no clue how he would reply.

Fred thought it over. "Not blindly. Like, not if I ordered her to break the law."

I recalled Danielle's comment about throwing her out. "Did your pastor really say that if she doesn't obey, you should divorce her?"

He cleared his throat. "Not exactly."

"Fred!" prompted his wife.

"He implied it," he conceded.

"Isn't marriage sacred?" I'd heard the term "the sanctity of marriage" at church, which I'd attended occasionally when Mom was alive. Since her death when I was thirteen, neither Dad nor I had gone back. "Shouldn't your goal be to work with Danielle to save your relationship?"

He ducked his head. "I don't like fighting with her, but Pastor Vald makes good points."

"That infertility is a punishment?" I said. "For the record, most of the cases I treat are unrelated to behavior."

"I've been praying and atoning for more than ten years," Danielle put in. "Surely God's forgiven me by now."

"Then why are we being punished again?" her husband countered. "The money that could have paid for a surrogate is gone. According to Pastor Vald, that indicates God still considers us sinners."

"You mean, considers *me* a sinner!"

"Wait a minute." Tory broke her bystander's silence. "This preacher, after discovering Mrs. Jeffers is no longer an heiress, advised you to you dump her?"

I had to admit, I hadn't made the connection. Kudos to Tory.

Fred's forehead wrinkled. "The two things aren't related."

"Are you sure?" Danielle seized on the idea. "He's always pushing for donations to build a real church."

"He isn't trying to break up our marriage because your mom lost her money." Fred drew back indignantly. "That would be immoral."

"More immoral than urging you to dump her if she doesn't knuckle under?" Tory was working up a head of steam.

"Down, girl," I muttered.

She winced. "Sorry," she told the Jefferses.

"He didn't mean it like that." Fred was too caught up in his mental turmoil to pay her much heed. "I don't want to lose you, honey."

"We have to find a new church," his wife said. "One where the minister acts like a Christian."

They were both breathing hard. Across the store, the young couple approached the checkout, their cart piled with towels.

"I have to think about this," Fred said.

"Sleep on it and call me tomorrow." Danielle swung around.

"Wait! Where will you stay?"

She called to the customers that she'd be right there. "A motel. Or Doreen's place. I'm sure she'll take me in."

His fists bunched. "You're not sleeping in that den of... whatever."

"It isn't your decision."

"We have to draw the line somewhere."

They'd reached an impasse. Someone had to break it. "We have a spare bedroom," I said.

"She can stay with us," Tory agreed.

"Us?" Fred's suspicion dropped over me like a giant net. "You're living together?"

Oh, great, we were about to be added to his list of

wrongdoers. "Not like that," I said. "My father-in-law, Tory's dad, also lives there. We have a fourth bedroom, if Danielle's interested."

"I suppose that would be all right," he said.

"Thank you," Danielle said in my direction. "Now I have customers waiting."

After she finished serving the young couple, we met her near the checkout. She had a condition for Fred, she announced. If by tomorrow he refused to compromise, she'd move out permanently.

She was quaking but resolute. I quashed the impulse to warn her against risking her marriage on an ultimatum, because there really might not be a future for them if Fred refused to meet her halfway. Also, I understood how hard it must be for her to stand firm.

Her husband ducked his head. "I'll see you in the morning."

I provided them both with my address. "The store closes at seven," Danielle said. "I'll pick up a change of clothes and come over. Thank you, Dr. Darcy. Ms. Golden."

"Very generous," Fred muttered.

"You're welcome."

Outside, Tory complimented me on the invitation. "I know how much you value your privacy."

"It's only one night," I said, "What did you learn from her before Fred barged in?"

"I'll tell you at home." Her sly grin reminded me that she got a kick out of keeping me off-balance. Mischievous, Lydia used to call her. Sometimes fondly, sometimes not.

Since Morris was catering a special event, I nibbled on leftovers until Tory arrived with a sack of hamburgers and fries. Pleasant surprise.

She filled me in as we ate. Danielle had shared background on Fred. He'd grown up in a small ranching community in

Wyoming, the middle child of seven. His parents were rigidly religious, with a sub-zero emotional chill factor.

"What I can't figure out is why he married someone with her personal history." Tory scooped a fry through a puddle of ketchup. "I mean, given his Neanderthal perspective."

"Because she's warm and kind, the opposite of his refrigerator parents," I said over a tankard of dark ale. I limit myself to one drink per night, since you never know when you might have to perform surgery.

"You think he'll compromise?"

"If he doesn't, he's a fool." The same, in my opinion, went for Keith, except that unlike Fred, he'd already crossed a line too far. Or too wide. Or both.

Danielle arrived about eight. Red hair wound in a bun and a small tote in hand, she had an air of fragility, and her shoulders drooped with weariness.

She'd already eaten dinner, she assured us. Despite the early hour, she was ready to go to bed and read her email.

"Oh, I nearly forgot." She paused behind Tory on the staircase. "Remember on Sunday, we discussed whether Mom might have gotten confused about her meds?"

"Yes?" From the hall, I regarded her encouragingly.

"Well, she *did* get confused sometimes."

"For example?"

She set her case on the step. "Right after Dee Marie died, when we thought it was from the asthma, Mom blamed herself for smoking when we were little. Because my sister was smaller and frailer than Doreen and me, Mom spent more time with her. That means she had more exposure to the cigarettes."

"If Dee Marie's lungs were less developed, she'd have been at higher risk for asthma in any event," I said. "But second-hand smoke could have increased her vulnerability."

"That wasn't the weird part," Danielle said. "While she was

beating up on herself, Mom mentioned heart defects. None of us had heart problems."

"Did she mean your father's stroke?" Surely Winston's own habit of lighting up had affected him more. I recalled seeing him sneak a cigarette on the lunchroom patio even though, as an anesthesiologist, he must have been aware that smokers run a higher risk of complications during surgery. People aren't always rational. Maybe I should say, aren't *often* rational.

"I didn't get that impression. But who knows?" She picked up the case. "Good night, Dr. Darcy."

"Good night." More than ever, I wished I had Malerie's missing file and the secrets it might contain.

On Wednesday, Fred arrived at 6 a.m. "Where's my wife?" he demanded.

"Right here." Wrapped in a robe, Danielle hurried down the stairs.

"I called your sister. Woke her up," he said. "I told her to find a neutral officiant. She already had a person in mind who was fine with me."

He'd covered a lot of topics in what sounded like a single breath. The underlying message was that he missed his wife far more than he would miss Pastor Vald.

"Is it okay if he comes in?" Danielle asked me.

"Sure." I waved toward the kitchen, from which wafted the scent of fresh brew. I'd remembered to fix it last night and set the timer for 5 a.m. "Help yourselves to coffee." Neither of my housemates appeared to be up yet.

Their thanks accompanied me upstairs. Leaving them to talk, I showered and dressed.

When I descended, the pair sat at the table, holding hands like newlyweds. Tory was fixing herself a bowl of cereal. No sign of Morris.

"I figured out what put a bee in my bonnet," Fred said when

he spotted me. "I hadn't been honest with myself how much I was counting on that inheritance until it vanished. That's no excuse for taking it out on my wife, though."

They soon departed, after telling me the ceremony and burial were scheduled for 1 p.m. Saturday at Safe Harbor Memorial Garden. "It's outdoors. Pray for good weather," Fred said cheerily.

"Let's hope." That's my standard response to such a request, since praying isn't part of my repertoire.

How often does a good deed bear results before you've eaten breakfast? If I weren't aware that whistling irritates people, I'd have produced a happy tune. Or attempted one.

"You'll be at the service too, right?" I asked Tory after they left.

"I could hardly miss it." To my questioning look, she said, "Eric, the killer almost always attends the funeral."

Just like that, my self-congratulatory mood disappeared.

CHAPTER THIRTEEN

Is there such a thing as a perfect day for a funeral? If so, Saturday surely qualified. By early afternoon, the temperature floated around 80 degrees, and light clouds diffused enough sunshine to avoid glare.

From a parking lot near the Memorial Garden's main building, Tory and I followed a meandering paved drive toward a canopy erected on the grass. Morris had reluctantly bowed out. He had meals to prepare for that night, with Billie's assistance. They'd be making deliveries together until she regained her confidence.

The rolling lawn was set with flat gravestones, some of which sported orange-and-black bouquets, pumpkins and skulls. After a startled moment, I recalled that the first of November, only a few days off, was *Día de los Muertos*, Day of the Dead. It's a holiday when Hispanic families traditionally clean and decorate the graves of loved ones. Apparently they incorporate Halloween decorations, as well.

A knot in my stomach reminded me that Lydia's grave lay halfway around the globe. Had she known when she wrote her will shortly before traveling that she would die in Israel? Perhaps she'd been uncertain of her intent until the instant when she leaped or fell from the cliff.

Tory had arranged the interment, where she, the tour guide and a few unidentified people had been the only mourners. I donated money to a private organization called a *chevra kadisha* or holy society to maintain the gravesite.

Someday, I would go to Israel to honor her memory. That might dispel my lingering pain and bitterness—or intensify it. I wasn't ready to find out which.

As we drew closer to the canopy, vehicles lined the narrow roadway, forcing us to walk on the grass. Except for a few folks visiting other graves, most people—close to fifty of them, I estimated—were taking places on the folding chairs.

A young-ish couple in dark clothing was paying a lot of attention to the crowd. "Cops?" I asked.

Tory nodded. "Yeah. There's Keith." He stood in a huddle with Malerie's daughters and their partners. A bandage slanted across Doreen's forehead. "Hey, what happened to her?"

Despite a tightening in my chest, I tried not to overreact as we hurried over. "Was there an accident?"

"Someone tried to kill her." Heather's arm encircled her girlfriend's waist.

Tory stiffened. "I wish you'd called me."

I wished I hadn't been so focused on the past that I'd ignored the possibility of danger to Malerie's surviving daughters. "Who? When?"

"Yesterday," Doreen said. "I didn't see who it was. All I could think was, oh, God, am I next?"

Keith, imposing in a dark suit, made room for Tory and me in the small group. "She was pulling out of a parking lot when a chunk of cement hit her windshield." Based on his impassive expression, I guessed he was reserving judgment as to the circumstances or intent.

"Is it possible the chunk flew up by accident?" I asked.

"That's a hell of a coincidence," Heather flared. "She nearly crashed into a bus on the boulevard."

"Instead, I hit the curb and wrecked a tire," Doreen grumbled. "Not to mention banging my head."

"I keep telling you to fasten your seatbelt!" Danielle scolded.

"Yeah. From now on," her sister said.

"We're seeking witnesses. Meanwhile, we'll take precautions." Keith must have meant the plainclothes officers.

"Where did this happen?" Tory asked.

Doreen explained that she'd been at the Oahu Lane Funeral Home on Safe Harbor Boulevard, adjacent to the animal shelter, which she'd also visited. The compromise candidate to conduct today's service was the shelter's director, who often conducted funerals for pets. The odd choice would no doubt have appealed to Malerie.

Once again, a murder attempt might have been disguised as an accident. Another coincidence teased my brain. Malerie had spotted the supposed quadruplet boarding a bus, and this attack had occurred near one. Had the red-haired imposter, if that's what she was, thrown the cement?

"Did you see anyone suspicious?" I stopped short of adding, "Such as a woman who could pass for you or Danielle." It sounded nutty. Also, putting such an idea in Doreen's head could distort her testimony.

"I was too dazed to notice," she said. "The road was full of rush hour traffic. But guess who stopped to *help*?" The last word quivered with sarcasm.

Heather leaped in. "Rafe. Pure chance that he was passing, right?"

Keith maintained a watchful silence. No doubt he'd already interviewed the relevant parties, but you never knew what might slip out.

"How many people were aware that you planned to visit the funeral home?" Tory asked.

"Anybody who'd read that the funeral was today could have deduced I'd be finalizing the arrangements," Doreen said. "We posted it on Mom's Facebook page." They must have left the page active for the short term.

"I'd have been there, too, if we hadn't had a sale at the store," Danielle noted. "We're short-staffed and since I'm the manager, I had to stick around."

"Until these crimes are solved, I'm driving you to work." As a self-employed computer consultant, Fred had a flexible schedule.

"Thanks, honey." Danielle smiled up at him. Peace had been restored between them, I was glad to see.

"The more I think about it, the more I wonder how much Rafe had to do with our money disappearing," Fred went on. "As an estate attorney, he deals with financial affairs. If anyone would be savvy about hiding funds, it would be him, right, Heather?"

Doreen's companion hesitated, as if expecting a follow-up zinger. When none materialized, she said, "It's possible."

"As executor, the guy has free rein to cover his tracks," Fred told Keith. "Are you pursuing that angle?"

My friend's jaw twitched. "I can't discuss that."

My focus returned to Doreen. "Did Rafe take you to the hospital?"

"You think she's stupid enough to get in his car?" Heather demanded.

"It's not a deep gash," Doreen said. "The paramedics took me to the ER, just in case, but there's no concussion."

"Thank goodness her air bag didn't inflate and break her ribs," Heather steamed. "Those damn devices were designed by men for other men. They're a threat to short women."

Doreen wasn't especially short. However, Heather barely reached her shoulder, and she was correct about the danger. I advise patients to sit at least ten inches from the steering wheel. Although studies have shown air bags to be generally safe for pregnant women, mothers-to-be should adjust the steering wheel to allow a ten-inch margin from the breastbone and be sure to wear seatbelts.

Sandy approached. In a black dress, the housekeeper appeared paler than usual. "Sorry to interrupt, but the funeral director suggested the family take their seats in the front row."

Aside from Keith, Tory and me, the group dispersed. As we talked, most of the chairs had filled up with neighbors and a sprinkling of hospital staff. I also recognized Malerie's sister-in-law Eunice in her wheelchair, accompanied by her husband.

They faced a gold-trimmed white casket flanked by a giant spray of flowers. Near the coffin stood a man in a charcoal suit and a tall, gray-haired woman. "Who're they?" I asked Keith.

"He's the funeral director," he said. "She's the officiant."

"Name of Ilsa Ivy," Tory added.

The incident with Doreen nagged at me. "You don't seriously believe Rafe chucked a concrete block into Doreen's windshield, do you?"

Keith continued to survey the surroundings.

"He can't discuss..." Tory said dryly.

"An ongoing..." Keith dropped in.

"Investigation," I finished.

"Glad we agree," he said.

Tory gazed past him. "Who's the mystery lady?" She indicated a woman in a form-fitting black dress and matching floppy hat with a wide brim.

"Oh, hell. It's Soraya Montenegro. I hoped we could keep the vultures out of this." Keith trudged toward her.

"I recognize the name," Tory told me. "Reporter for *The Safe*

Harbor Journal."

The woman appeared to be viewing the scene through her phone camera. She was attractive, with creamy olive skin and a spectacular shape. Also spectacularly poor taste if she intended to take ghoulish photos.

Looking up, she flashed a smile at Keith. A subtle squaring of the shoulders marked my friend's reaction to her very feminine presence.

"He's such an alley cat," Tory said.

"He hasn't done anything," I pointed out.

"Today."

"Jealous?" I should have kept my mouth shut. "Never mind. I hate to think of him as a player."

"Because he's your pal?"

"Because you deserve better." Also, I believed he genuinely wanted to patch up their relationship, if he could figure out how.

Deciding I'd shot my mouth off enough, I joined Tory in observing Soraya and Keith conduct their newshound-vs.-cop interplay. The glinting teeth (hers), the angling hips (his), the occasional audible phrase: "mother and daughter murders" (her again), "respect the family's privacy" (him).

"No matter what he says, she'll whip up a soap opera for her readers," Tory snarled. "Why doesn't anyone just report the news any more?"

"Hard to do without solid info." I hadn't meant to defend the woman. In truth, I despise the media hype that treats victims' pain as entertainment. There weren't any TV cameras in evidence, but if Soraya beat the drum loudly enough about the mother-and-child murders, there soon would be.

The animal lady advanced to the microphone. She had an erect spine and a commanding manner.

"I'm Ilsa Ivy," she told the assembly. "On behalf of the

family, thank you for coming."

From the corner of my eye, I noted a man crossing the grass toward us. Medium height, dark-blue suit, thin face. If Rafe's goal had been to avoid confrontations, he'd timed his arrival well.

Keith went on the alert. But whether from concern about disrupting the service or awareness of the reporter's sharpened interest, he held his position.

"To paraphrase Shakespeare, I come to bury Malerie Abernathy, not to praise her," Ilsa's voice rang out as Rafe reached Tory and me. That struck me as a peculiar statement for a funeral.

"Where'd they find her?" Rafe muttered to me.

"She runs the animal shelter."

"Why am I not surprised?"

"She knows her literary references," Tory said.

"Before anyone drags me off, I don't plan to speak ill of Malerie, who was a wonderful volunteer at the Oahu Lane Animal Shelter," Ilsa continued. "To be honest, Malerie could get cranky, she could be high-handed and she could deliver a tongue-lashing with the best of us. She was also funny, warm-hearted and occasionally generous, although let's not exaggerate." A ripple of laughter ran through the gathering.

"This is the strangest eulogy I ever heard," Rafe said quietly.

"I've always been glad God doesn't expect us to be perfect," Ilsa said. "Only to do our best, which I believe Malerie did. Let me tell you a little about her life, which her daughters have shared with me."

She ran through the highlights: Born sixty years ago to loving parents who died when she was in college and whose illnesses inspired her to enter the nursing profession. Married at thirty-one to widower Winston Abernathy—no mention of the previous affair, of course—followed by the birth of triplets.

Widowed four years ago, and mourning the death of her daughter Dee Marie six months earlier.

At his wife's name, Rafe's breathing rasped. "Does it ever stop hurting?"

"No." To be accurate, I added, "Not yet, anyway." And probably never.

Ilsa concluded by introducing Doreen. As she took the microphone, a stray sunbeam picked out the white bandage on her forehead until it appeared to glow. Simultaneously, her gaze lit on Rafe.

"What the hell are you doing here?" she cried.

A rustle ran through the crowd as people shifted to stare at us. Near Keith, Soraya lifted her phone again. Taking a picture?

"Sorry," Doreen told the crowd. "I, um, had an accident yesterday and my head's hurting. Please don't attack my brother-in-law. He carries a gun."

"Left it at home," Rafe called.

Soraya angled her phone. I was grateful when Keith blocked her view and, after an apology, she dropped the cell in her purse.

Doreen appeared stuck for words, and Danielle sat frozen. Before the silence could lengthen further, Sandy stepped to the mic.

"Hi, I'm Sandy Faye Miller," she said. "I met Malerie more than thirty years ago when we worked together at the hospital. I'd had a rough childhood and was painfully shy. Malerie became the friend I desperately needed."

As she recounted fond memories, the daughters regained their composure. Soon they were able to speak about their mother with only a few throat-clearing pauses.

Rafe fidgeted. I hoped he didn't plan to march up there and deliver an off-the-wall statement of his own. Instead, he addressed me in a low tone.

"I guess you heard about the incident with Doreen," he said. "I mean, the part where I stopped to check on her, fool that I am. Never occurred to me she'd assume it was my fault."

Although I disliked speaking during the service, he deserved a response. "The police cleared you, right?"

"Took them half an hour." He scowled in Keith's direction. "I was on my way home from the courthouse in Santa Ana, which they confirmed. That didn't one hundred percent preclude my running around like a maniac smashing windshields, but they let me go."

"Did you observe anyone suspicious in the area?" Tory asked.

"You sound like a cop." His mouth curved. "I forgot—you're the PI. No, I was too busy watching my sister-in-law crash into the curb and barely miss a bus."

"Were there passengers boarding?" I asked. "Anyone you recognized?" *Such as a ringer for the triplets?*

Rafe frowned. "You think a passenger threw the rock?"

"Could they have?"

"Dunno. The bus pulled out as I got there," he said. "I was floored when Doreen practically accused me. We got along fine the day before."

"What happened on Thursday?" I asked.

"The three of us went through the house and listed the valuables. Everyone was quite civil."

"What kind of valuables?" Tory asked.

"TVs, cappuccino machine, jewelry."

"Did they notice any items missing?" I asked.

"Her photo albums. I can't imagine who'd want those." He folded his arms and regarded the front, where Danielle was describing how her mother used to take her to ballet lessons and cheer at her recitals.

"To her, I was Pavlova reincarnated." She smiled tearfully.

"I let her down on that score."

"Any luck tracing the money?" Tory murmured to Rafe.

"Persistent, aren't you?"

"Doing my job."

He shrugged. "Better than the police. All they've done is search for evidence to pin this on me."

I wasn't convinced of that. But I didn't dispute how it might seem from Rafe's perspective.

By the casket, the funeral director wished everyone a safe journey home. Although families often hold a post-funeral gathering, they hadn't scheduled one today.

"So, what *have* you learned about the missing money?" Tory pressed.

"That Malerie's bookkeeping was haphazard." Rafe ignored the curious faces of mourners as they passed us en route to their cars. "She paid some bills in cash and others on line. A few of the amounts appear inappropriately large."

"Surely you can tell who the payees were," Tory said.

"They might not all have been legitimate. Also, it appears she gambled on Internet stock tips," Rafe said. "Plus she made a big investment in a local company, a medical diagnostics firm."

"How big?" I asked.

"Several hundred thousand dollars."

"Wow," Tory said. "What happened to it?"

"The firm went belly up due to mismanagement. I haven't determined who or what inspired her to invest. Or, more importantly, who benefited."

"How long has she been investing like this?" Tory was taking notes.

"From what Dee Marie told me, the papers she was sorting dated to soon after Winston died. However, the diagnostics business was just a few months ago."

"Do you get the sense we're circling a dark secret from the

past?" I asked. "And that whenever someone gets close, they end up dead?"

"If you keep digging, you'd better watch out, doc," Rafe advised. "Ever consider that you could be in danger?"

My throat clamped. No, I hadn't.

"Why do you mention it?" Tory's cool tone centered me.

"I'm worried for my own sake, too." Rafe's voice was barely audible above the chatter and stirrings around us.

"Why?"

A long breath swelled his narrow chest. "Earlier this afternoon, I ran across a file I didn't recognize. Maybe I shouldn't tell you, but I have to trust someone. And it sure as hell won't be the police."

He had my full attention. "What kind of file?"

"Right before I left the house, I was backing up material for a client." He checked his watch. "In fact, he and I are meeting in half an hour. Anyway, while I was on the cloud, I spotted an unfamiliar file name. It might be nothing. Or else my wife put it there."

Until now, as far as I knew, everyone had believed all Dee Marie's records were stolen. The possibility of an on-line backup riveted me.

"Why didn't it surface before?" Tory asked.

"I had no idea she ever copied files onto my account. Both my laptop and my cloud storage are password-protected, but I could have left them open when I was working at home," he said. "I'd been lecturing her about getting cloud storage of her own. Maybe she decided to borrow mine."

"You have to tell Detective Sparks," Tory said.

"I will, if it does turn out to be her notes. However, it might be a client file that I misnamed."

"If it's hers..." My throat closed again.

"Then the information probably got her killed." With a

touch of melodrama, Rafe added, "And if I'm not careful, that file might get me killed, too."

"Lower your voice," Tory hissed.

Belatedly, he—and I—took note of our surroundings. And spotted Heather a few feet away, staring at us.

CHAPTER FOURTEEN

"Crap," Rafe said. "Damn eavesdropper."

Heather appeared on the verge of snapping back at him, until a gentle hand on her arm—Sandy's—drew her into reluctant retreat. She didn't go far. Just far enough to join Doreen, Fred and Danielle, to whom she spoke with angry animation accompanied by pointing in our direction.

"Now the whole world has me in its sights," Rafe snarled.

"Let's talk to Detective Sparks," Tory said. "He can provide protection while you review the file."

A few dozen yards away, the object of her recommendation was fending off the teasing remarks of Soraya Montenegro. I knew Keith well enough to read his discomfort, and hoped Tory did, too.

"No way." Rafe checked his watch. "I'll have to put pedal to the metal to keep my appointment, and this client's a stickler. Besides which, who'll protect me from that damn cop? All he wants is a reason to lock me up."

"Don't underestimate him." That couldn't have been easy for Tory to say.

"Most likely, I simply forgot the file name and it's privileged information about a client," Rafe retorted. "Hell, I'll be safe enough. My alarm's set and I won't let anyone in until my sister brings dinner."

I'd almost forgotten Rafe was one of Morris's clients. "Be careful." What a useless comment. Couldn't stop myself.

Tory's lips thinned. She believed in following procedure, and that meant sharing this situation with Keith. "Seriously, sir, I advise you to confide in Detective Sparks."

"No, thanks." The thin man scowled. "This may not be evidence at all. And for now, it's safe on the cloud."

Was information safe on the cloud? I'd received notices from two major corporations in the past year that my data had been hacked. Still, there was no indication that Malerie's killer was a cyber sleuth.

"I'm not comfortable..." Tory began.

"I appreciate your concern," Rafe said. "Eric, if I find anything, I'll send you a copy of the file."

I remembered his remark about my being in danger. I'm not a coward—nor a fool either. "Send copies far and wide."

"Good idea."

Rafe double-timed toward his car. Tory hurried off to question attendees before they scattered.

I wished there were a post-funeral gathering. Not only for the emotional release, but also to hear what the family thought of Rafe's discovery. Whether Heather was spinning it in self-serving fashion. Or if Fred considered this a ploy on Rafe's part.

It was hard to fathom why Rafe would invent a mystery file to cover his tracks. Still, I'm astonished by the scams and quasi-legal maneuverings that Tory and Keith gripe about. I wish I knew how to be devious in order to understand people who are.

Since we'd arrived in Tory's car and her inquiries could be lengthy, I considered who I might cadge a ride from. Keith was obviously busy. Also, alone with my friend, it would be hard not to betray Rafe's confidence. Perhaps I *should* do that, for Rafe's safety as well as for the sake of the investigation.

As I was weighing options, a man halted beside me. Short like his father, with curly brown hair like his sister, Barry Golden had just been elected my chauffeur. That's my brother-in-law's knack: he tends to be the right guy in the right place at the right time, usually without intending to.

"What are you doing here?" I asked. Not the friendliest greeting, especially when I was about to request a favor, but his presence puzzled me.

"My entire family is caught up in this case. I was curious." He cocked his head at me. "Also, I have an assignment from Dad. Hear me out."

"Any chance we can discuss this while you drive me home?"

"Tory abandoned you?"

A survey of the scene revealed her speaking intently with Ilsa Ivy. "Either she's conducting an interview or planning to adopt a pet."

"No pets. She had a hamster once. Didn't realize they only live two or three years." As he spoke, Barry strolled along the grass beside me. "She never recovered from the trauma of finding its furry little body."

"Which fails to explain why she chose a career that might require shooting someone," I observed.

"That's different. She loved Betty," Barry said.

"The hamster's name was Betty?"

"It was brown."

The reference piqued my appetite. Too bad Morris wouldn't be arriving with the promised leftovers until six. I hoped he'd fixed Brown Betty for dessert, since the apple dish was popular with his customers.

We reached an ancient van that bore traces of psychedelic paint from its former hippie owner. Inside, a slip cover in a noxious shade of green hid what I guessed were tears in the seat cushions.

Never mind the common belief that doctors are rich. Barely past his residency in urology, Barry staggered beneath massive student loans.

"What's Morris's assignment?" I asked as he navigated out of the cemetery.

We turned south on Industrial Way. "Starts with thanks."

"Ends with giving." What else had I expected?"

"Dad's concerned about you sinking into a depression." Barry delivered that piece of non-news with the enthusiasm of a weatherman predicting drizzle.

"I'm not depressed, just grumpy."

"Well, if we can't celebrate Thanksgiving at your house, we'll either have to squeeze into Dad's tiny tasting room or my apartment, which isn't much bigger." When I didn't respond, Barry added, "My roommate's dropping hints that his entire family may show up."

"Could be fun."

"Not from the way he describes them." He grunted. "By the way, does this street go through? I can't remember."

"No."

"Oops." Barry swung onto a road that carried us past the City Hall complex, including the two-story stucco police department. Guilt descended. Keith really ought to hear that Dee Marie's notes might be floating around in cyberspace. Maybe I should call him.

But what good would it do now? Rafe had been dead set—*pick another term, Eric*—determined to meet with his appointed client. Besides, the file might contain only privileged information irrelevant to the case.

Barry took a wandering route through side streets. Just when I began to think we'd have to retrace our path, we emerged onto Safe Harbor Boulevard. "Any chance of changing your mind about Thanksgiving?"

"No."

"Okay, duty done." Cheerfully, my brother-in-law switched subjects. "How's my sister surviving the break-up?"

"With bad grace," I conceded.

"And Keith?"

"No grace at all."

At the house, Barry declined my invitation to come inside and headed off, having dispatched his duty with tact and humor. As I said, my favorite of Lydia's relatives.

Yet fond as I was of Morris and his offspring, they didn't feel like my family. Not the way Lydia had been.

After Barry departed, I sprawled on the couch in the downstairs den to catch up on medical journals. Instead, fragments from the funeral drifted through my mind: mourners in dark clothing, that reporter flirting with Keith, the jarring sight of skulls and orange-and-black wreaths.

Three years ago, Halloween had fallen during a sad autumn, as my father's weak heart defied the efforts of medical science. He had spent most evenings watching videos of my childhood and my mother, by then nearly twenty years gone. His face had become more deeply lined with every passing day.

Then Lydia, infused with a merry spirit that sprang unexpectedly from her restless depths, whipped into action. With the cooperation of more friends than I'd known she possessed, she created a narrative for our house. Here a comic book artist had lived and died, the story went, returning from beyond the grave on Halloween to bring his creations to life.

She constructed a path through the great room and this den, punctuated by manikins emerging from comic-book blowups. By the holiday eve, I scarcely recognized the familiar contours, thanks to mirrors, fake spiderwebs and a rented fog machine. Aided by eerie lights and noises, a handful of people in superhero getups conspired to thrill friends, neighbors and their children.

Costumed as Spiderman and flanked by grimacing pumpkins, I greeted our guests on the porch with flashlights and instructions. Dad and Morris presided over a kitchen redolent of apple cider and cinnamon, and well supplied with pastries and candies. Tory supervised a dining room from which the table had been removed, where survivors of the haunted trail could dance to "The Monster Mash" and similar selections.

Wearing a dreamy pastel gown and wielding a fairy-princess scepter, Lydia had flitted through the rooms, replacing burned-out green bulbs, comforting a startled preschooler and retrieving a lost toddler. What a wonderful mother she would be, I thought on that night when all futures seemed possible.

To me, she'd been the star of the event, with the rest of us in supporting roles. That had felt natural, because I visualized our life together as a movie with her name above the title and everyone else, including me, in the credits that scroll at the end.

After the last friend had departed and the food been tucked away, Lydia and I had made love with a freedom that bordered on delirium. I could have sworn we hovered above the bed, laughing so loud that Dad must have heard us from the opposite end of the house.

For weeks afterward, his melancholy lifted and his strength returned. We celebrated a joyful Thanksgiving.

In December, he died. Lydia and I scattered Dad's ashes at sea, as he'd requested. Now I wished I had a grave to visit. For each of them.

The doorbell broke into my melancholy thoughts. Downstairs, I admitted an ill-tempered homicide detective.

My watch indicated that six o'clock had passed. "If you're looking for dinner, Morris is late," I informed him.

Keith shambled into the great room. "Isn't Tory back yet? I thought she left ahead of me."

"Neither Golden has arrived."

"Just as well."

"Why?" Knowing his bottomless appetite, I'd assumed he was eager for dinner.

Plopping onto the sofa, Keith draped his long legs over the arm. "You're good at keeping confidences, right?"

"I try."

"I'd like to know how Tory reacted to that reporter cozying up to me. And don't tell her I asked." His semi-reclining position altered his appearance, adding a touch of loose flesh along the jaw and creases around the eyes. I realized—sucker punch—that he was nearing middle age. Which meant *we* were nearing middle age.

Stay on topic, Eric. "You mean, was she jealous?"

"Yes."

"She plays her cards close," I said carefully.

"You aren't normally this evasive." Keith's eyes hardened. "Is something going on between you two?"

Excuse me? "Not even close. She accused me of having a giant ego. I think she's mad because I treat her like a kid sister."

"Yes, you do, and it annoys the hell out of her. She had a raging crush on you in high school."

"You're making that up."

"That's among the reasons I never went after her," Keith said.

"Plus you were dating Catherine." Keith's girlfriend, she of the long brown hair, breezy manner and taste for designer fashions, had dropped him after graduation to pursue a business degree and a man who earned more than a cop's salary. "Who broke your heart right after the prom."

"She bruised my pride more than my heart." My friend was in an unusually introspective mood. For him as well as me, the funeral must have churned up the past. "She announced I wasn't good enough for her. It threw me."

"You?" Insecurity and Keith move in different circles.

"Yeah, for five minutes," he remarked. "I hear she's been divorced twice."

"Ever consider calling her?"

"Not even slightly," he said. "I need a woman who gets me. Who has the same taste in action movies, doesn't waste time on touchy-feely crap, who's physical, even the way she makes love."

"TMI," I said. Too much information.

"It's that soul mate business," Keith summarized.

I caught his drift. "As in, Tory."

"Yeah." He cleared his throat. "I expected her to be with me all the way, to understand if I occasionally blow off steam."

"You mean, like cheating on her?"

"It's human nature. Except for you, maybe."

The adjectives I'd applied to him in English class hadn't included clueless, but they should have. "So it would be fine if she cheated, too?"

"The hell it would!"

"I thought you and Tory had the same world view."

"Women are different." He didn't sound convinced.

"Partners have to be able to count on each other," I said. "To establish a circle of trust that excludes everyone else."

"In other words, I violated her trust," he said.

"You stabbed her in the back."

"Damn. How do I fix this?" Keith peered at me as if asking for the formula to a tough algebra problem.

"When people get married, it's their job to be their

partner's best friend." That was what I'd believed, and for five years, it had worked.

"I get that," he said impatiently.

"That means supporting each other." I stuck to the steady tone I'd heard our staff psychologist use in addressing skeptical groups. "Listening. Encouraging. Sharing the pain when they fail without belittling their disappointment."

"Being there for them." Keith flung his head back against the arm of the sofa. "How many times have I heard that about relationships?"

"Not enough for it to sink in, apparently." I sneaked a glance at my phone in case I'd missed a text or an email. By now, Rafe should be home eating dinner and reading the mystery file. No message.

"I can always count on you to lay it on the line."

"Well?"

He swung his legs around and sat up. Despite the evening shadows invading the great room, I saw a light go on in my friend's eyes. "You really believe it will do the trick?"

"It isn't a trick," I said.

"I hate that touchy-feely crap, but not as much as I hate losing her," Keith said.

"Good." With every flick of the digital readout, my uneasiness mounted. "There's something I should tell you. It's about Rafe."

"Regarding whatever you were discussing today?"

"Yes." Footsteps approaching from the hall cut me off.

Tory halted, her gaze sweeping across her ex-boyfriend on the couch and me near the tall mullioned windows. "Where's Dad?" she asked me.

"I wish I knew." Morris should have returned by now from delivering meals with Billie.

"Where've you been?" Keith queried.

"Interviewing people." She flicked a speck from her dark-blue suit jacket.

"Have a seat." He patted the couch beside him. "You can fill me in while we wait for your father."

Discarding her oversize purse, Tory sank into an armchair instead. "It occurred to me that if Mrs. Abernathy gabbed about her investments to other volunteers, Mrs. Ivy might have overheard."

A flicker of the eyelids marked Keith's reaction. I interpreted it to mean he wished he'd thought of that. "Good work, Tory. Did she?"

My sister-in-law slipped off her pumps. "A couple of months ago, Mrs. Abernathy urged her to put money into a medical diagnostics firm. She tossed around adjectives like dynamic and innovative."

Just as Rafe had mentioned. But he hadn't learned where the tip came from. "Did Malerie cite a source?"

"No."

"Did Mrs. Ivy invest?" Keith's fingers flexed as if to move pieces around on a bulletin board, except that these days police use a computer program instead of a physical display.

"No. She claims she can smell a scam a mile away."

Malerie had lost several hundred thousand dollars within the past few months. Since this investment dated from after Dee Marie's murder, it couldn't be connected to Rafe's mystery file. Unless, that is, the tip had come from the same person who'd been ruining the Abernathy finances all along.

I was mulling the implications when I heard the front door open. A second later, Tory called out, "Dad! What happened?"

A sorry version of my father-in-law, clothes wrinkled and face shiny with sweat, stood staring at Keith. "Oh, lord, it's you." He drew in a deep, shuddery breath and extended his hands, wrists together. "You might as well arrest me now."

CHAPTER FIFTEEN

"Arrest you?" Keith echoed. "What have you done?"

Morris began shaking. Tory hurried to grab his arm. "Sit down, Dad."

"I can't bear it."

"Bear what?"

"I can't believe it!" he cried as she led him to an armchair. "I've killed a client."

Keith catapulted to his feet. "Who? How?"

"Rafe Tibbets." Taking in our dismayed reactions, Morris hurried on. "My cooking must have killed him. He's allergic to peanuts. I can't figure it out—we're very careful. When Billie delivered the meal, he was fine. A few minutes later, after she came out to the van, we heard a crash. When we ran in, he'd collapsed on the floor."

This was a truly alarming development, since anaphylactic shock can be fatal if swelling blocks the airway. "What about his EpiPen?" I asked.

Morris's hands carved the air. "He must have been overcome too fast to use it. Billie injected him."

Grimly, Keith lifted his phone. "He's dead?"

145

"Unconscious. He hit his head when he fell."

"Where is he?"

"The paramedics took him to Heights View," my father-in-law rasped. Unlike Safe Harbor, that hospital has an emergency room. "Billie's with him."

"Are the police searching his house?" Keith demanded.

"No. The paramedics must have called them, because they showed up and took a report. Then they left."

Keith muttered angrily about the one-track minds of some patrol officers. "Did you remove or touch anything?"

"I think the paramedics took some of the food for testing," Morris said. "After they left, I locked up and finished the deliveries."

"You did what?" Tory said in dismay. "Dad..."

"Nobody else has a peanut allergy, so I didn't see how the food could hurt them, and I was late," Morris said weakly.

"You can't be sure it was peanuts," she said. "What if you poisoned your customers?"

"I ate a little of every item myself," he said. "And waited a few minutes. It was delicious. Cheese ravioli with steamed vegetables and Apple Brown Betty."

We regarded him open-mouthed. Of all the stupid risks! In his panic, he'd clung to his guiding principle: Never disappoint a customer.

It occurred to me that he'd fixed the dessert I'd dreamed about. But even if it hadn't been potentially poisoned, any leftovers had become evidence.

"What did you do next?" Keith stopped. "Hold on. I need to talk to you alone." In the heat of the moment, he'd forgotten to isolate the witness.

Morris barreled ahead. "I went back to my kitchen and searched for contaminants."

"What the hell were you thinking?" Fury suffused my

friend's face. Even Tory looked apprehensive.

"For what it's worth, I didn't find any."

"You might have destroyed evidence without realizing it!" Another instant and there'd be steam pouring from Keith's ears.

"Breathe," I told him.

"What?"

"Just do it."

A couple of long breaths cleared the fiery red from his cheeks. When Keith resumed addressing Morris, he was stern but calmer. "Do we have permission to search your property?"

"Of course." Morris fished out a key.

On his phone, Keith alerted his sergeant to the developments. He arranged for officers to secure Rafe's house and Morris's catering facility, and learned from the hospital's nursing supervisor that Rafe was unconscious but stable.

On TV, people suffer knocks in the head and wake up minutes later with a slight ache. In real life, head trauma can be deadly. If Rafe survived, he ran the risk of serious disabilities.

"Billie was in the house for several minutes when she delivered the meal?" Tory rocked from foot to foot. Clearly, like me, she was troubled by Billie's bad habit of being on the scene of possible murders. "Did you go in with her?"

"No," Morris said. "Why?"

"They were both out of your sight right before he collapsed? And again when she administered the shot?" Tory asked.

"Billie didn't do this," protested my father-in-law. "Rafe's her brother!"

Keith got off the phone. "Stop talking, all of you. Morris, wait for me upstairs in the library."

"Okay." Off he went with robotic stiffness.

Keith placed another call to assign an officer to guard the

victim. Rafe's sister was not to be allowed near him.

I didn't believe Billie had tried to kill her brother. According to Morris's story, she'd administered the epinephrine that might have saved him. But it was Keith's job to be cautious.

I also didn't believe that Morris had delivered a contaminated meal from carelessness. We now had two murders and another possible attack—two, if you counted the cement chunk that hit Doreen's windshield—each initially appearing to be an accident.

"I think whoever did this wanted that file," Tory said.

Keith frowned. "Mrs. Abernathy's file that was stolen from Eric?"

"No, Dee Marie's notes," I said. "Rafe told us at the funeral he stumbled across a file he didn't recognize among his cloud backups. I was about to explain that before Tory got here."

"You'd damn well better explain it now." Keith waved a hand in frustration. "Alone. Tory, you can provide your account later."

"I'll go check on Dad."

"No!"

When her jaw tensed, I braced for an argument. But he was right and she knew it. "I'll wait in the conservatory."

"The what?" Keith asked.

"Lydia's studio."

Once she was out of earshot, I described how Rafe had planned to view the unfamiliar file after his client appointment. Also how Heather had overheard the conversation, which she'd apparently relayed to the family.

"And no one alerted me. Now Rafe's unconscious," Keith raged. "His house has been unguarded. If he left his computer on, whoever did this has had plenty of opportunity to access it."

He was right. "I'm sorry."

"I'd better go interview Morris in case there's any information you two haven't contaminated."

It wasn't our fault he'd let the witness chatter away in front of us. He'd been as distracted by Morris's statements as we had. But I saw no point in reminding him of that.

Keith hurried upstairs. In the studio, I found Tory on a call with Doreen. "I'll keep you advised," Tory assured her client. "You and your sister should be very careful."

How? I wondered. They couldn't isolate themselves from everyone close to them. What if the killer was Heather or Fred or Sandy—or Doreen or Danielle?

Or a look-alike who might, at a glance, pass for either of them?

Shame flooded me. I might have prevented this latest tragedy had I not been so caught up in the belief that I'd been entrusted with a mission. Instead of reporting the existence of a suspicious file, I'd acted as if this were my case to investigate. Tory was right about my giant ego. Being a doctor didn't make me a superhero.

I went into the kitchen and scrambled half a dozen eggs to share with Tory and whoever else might be hungry. When she joined me, she reported that Doreen had been upset about her brother-in-law's injury and promised to spread the word to Danielle.

A few minutes later, after obtaining Tory's account of our conversation with Rafe, Keith departed for the hospital. Morris calmed a little when his daughter fixed him a cup of cocoa and settled him in front of a documentary series called *Dogs With Jobs*.

"He loves that show," she told me as we headed to Heights at Morris's request, to check on Billie.

Tory let me drive, since my M.D. sticker from Safe Harbor might prove useful. However, I've had no reason to seek admitting privileges at Heights, which long ago closed its maternity unit. In the rare event that a patient of mine lands there, I coordinate with a physician on staff. Rafe was not my patient, so any special treatment I received would be purely a courtesy.

Despite the lofty name, Heights occupies a flat site north of the freeway. The only upgrade to the forty-plus-year-old facility is a modern wing stuck on its butt.

I didn't push my luck by occupying a space reserved for doctors. Instead, I plucked a ticket from the machine—unlike Safe Harbor, Heights charges for parking—and puttered into the ramped structure.

Emergency rooms get busy late on Saturday nights, when alcohol, bad driving and gang shootings kick in. At seven p.m., however, the waiting room held only a scattering of people, including a fidgety Keith.

Shortly after we entered, a nurse with striking black hair and a name tag that read N. Petrakis, R.N., popped in from the hallway to hand him a wrapped sandwich and lidded cup. The smile lighting her face implied this was the lady of the fling.

Beside me, Tory's lip curled. "How sweet."

Catching sight of us, Keith froze. If I'd doubted the nurse's identity, his discomfort confirmed it.

"Thank goodness you're here." Billie Tibbets waylaid us from the side. A baseball cap hid her purple hair, which explained why I hadn't noticed her immediately. "They barred me from seeing my brother. I'm his next of kin and I should be in the loop. Now that cop's threatening to haul me down to the station."

No surprise there. "Have you agreed to an interview?"

"Are you kidding?" As her voice rose, we drew a quelling glance from Nurse Petrakis. "He wants to pin this on me. I didn't hurt my brother!"

"It's in your best interest to be straight with the police," Tory said.

"I don't care," Billie squealed. "I want out. Tell Morris I quit. I can't deliver another dinner."

"I don't blame you," I said. This had to be the deadliest catering job since the Romans fed Christians to the lions.

Ms. Petrakis stalked over, an electronic tablet held in front of her like a shield. "Please lower your voices."

Both Tory and Billie swung toward her with teeth bared. The startled woman retreated a pace.

Much as I sympathized with my companions, I have great respect for nurses. Also a certain irritation with Keith, who'd created this awkward situation.

"Hi, I'm Dr. Eric Darcy," I said. "From Safe Harbor."

The nurse frowned at the tablet. "You have a patient here?"

"Rafe Tibbets' late wife was my patient, and we've become friends." Only a slight exaggeration. "Billie here is his sister."

"Yes, I've been advised about her," came the cool response.

"And Tory is an investigator representing Rafe's sister-in-law," I finished. "We apologize for disrupting your E.R."

"Any change in his condition?" Billie asked.

Ms. Petrakis hesitated. But neither strict patient privacy rules nor the police ban on direct contact had changed Billie's status as Rafe's next of kin.

"The doctor ordered a CT scan to look for a skull fracture or bleeding," she said.

"Has the neurologist arrived?" I asked.

"She's on her way." To Billie, the nurse explained, "She'll evaluate the damage and decide whether surgery is required."

"That stupid tile in his kitchen," Billie said. "That's what he hit. It's as hard as a rock."

"Soft floor coverings don't hold up well in kitchens." The nurse cleared her throat. "But that's irrelevant."

Speaking of irrelevant, I automatically compared N. Petrakis (Natalie? Nora? Nadine?) with Tory. Black, straight hair woven into a chignon vs. shoulder-length brown waves; black eyes vs. green; and a few inches shorter—that was the nurse. Not the same physical type but both raised their chins boldly, braced for verbal combat. Also, both sneaked glances at Keith, Tory's aggrieved and Natalie/Nora/Nadine's speculative.

"Mind telling me your first name?" I asked.

"Narda," she said. "What's the subtext here? I'm missing something."

I was impressed by her use of "subtext." So, apparently, was Billie-the-English-grad. "Detective Sparks was sneaking around on Tory with you." To me, she noted, "Morris told me about him cheating with a nurse. The way she's been treating him, I figure it was her."

Among the waiting patients, heads turned. A few people leaned forward to hear better. Most continued playing games on their phones.

"You're his girlfriend?" Narda asked Tory.

"Used to be."

"He wasn't wearing a ring," the nurse said. "Anyway, a guy who's involved with a woman ought to act like it."

"You're right."

Tossing his sandwich wrappings in the trash, Keith stalked over. Whatever his thoughts about the two women's confrontation, I felt certain he had more serious matters in mind.

However, Nurse Petrakis beat him to the punch. "Were you dating this woman?" Her chin jerked toward Tory.

"Yes." He ducked his head. "Let's discuss this later, Narda."

"Fine. If I'm not too busy." Nostrils flaring, she marched away.

His gaze met Tory's. "I'm sorry."

"Yeah. Me, too."

He swung toward Billie. "Ms. Tibbets, I cut you some slack until you cooled off. Now I need for you to tell me what happened."

"At the risk of repeating myself—up yours, detective." As Billie faced him, I saw that the back of her T-shirt read: "Be yourself; everyone else is already taken.– Oscar Wilde."

Keith scowled. "Miss Tibbets, if your brother had trusted me with the information about finding an unidentified file, I might have prevented this."

"What file?" Billie asked.

"Let's discuss this privately."

"Not interested. I told you the whole story after I found Mrs. Abernathy, and what good did it do? You let the killer keep right on attacking people."

He blew out a frustrated breath. "Miss Tibbets, don't force my hand. I'd hate to have to arrest you."

"I'll sue!"

Just as I feared his head might explode, down the aisle swayed a vision in a black dress and hat. "Detective Sparks! Just the handsome fellow I was hoping to see."

"Not another one," Tory muttered.

"I haven't encouraged her, believe me." Keith's forehead creased in annoyance as the reporter swept to a halt. "Miss Montenegro, no comment."

Without missing a beat, Soraya targeted Billie. "You're Miss Tibbets, aren't you? I stopped by your brother's house and a neighbor told me he'd been injured. How is he? Did you see what happened?"

"You're interfering with a homicide investigation." Keith's simmering fury flamed toward her. "You're leaving the premises. If you butt in again, I'll arrest you. Got it?"

The reporter paled. "Okay, detective." She scurried through

the ER and out.

"As for you, Miss Tibbets..."

His obviously shredded patience must have resonated with Billie. "All right," she said. "I'll talk to you. On one condition."

His expression said *Oh, hell*. "What's that?"

"I want a witness." She pointed at me. "Him."

CHAPTER SIXTEEN

Keith shot me a discouraging glare. "I'm glad to help but I can't offer legal advice," I reminded Billie.

"You did fine last time," she said. "He wasn't in the way, was he, detective? Admit it."

After a tick of inner struggle, Keith yielded. "Ground rules. The doc listens and keeps his mouth shut."

"Fine by me," I said.

Tory promised to watch in case the reporter returned. She also, I was sure, intended to brief her father on the latest developments.

With Narda's permission, the three of us retreated to a private waiting room down the hall. Hospitals maintain these for families dealing with difficult situations.

After Keith offered Billie a drink, which she declined, we took seats around the small space. He activated his recorder, introduced himself, stated the time, date, and place, and identified those present.

I remained on alert. Although I didn't intend to interfere—Keith might be irked enough to take *me* into custody—I owed Billie my support, both for Morris's sake and for Rafe's.

Keith proceeded through the events of that afternoon and

evening. With only minor variations, she repeated what Morris had told us earlier: that she'd heard her brother fall, raced inside and injected him with medication.

"He hadn't locked the door?"

She shrugged. "I have a key."

"And you know the alarm code?"

"Sure."

"But you were with Morris all day," I pointed out, before recalling that I was here as a witness only. "Oh. Sorry."

"That's right," she said.

Keith gritted his teeth. If he weren't careful, he'd have a major dental bill before this case was over.

Billie continued her account. Only she and Morris had handled the food, she told us. Rafe had been home when they arrived, and hadn't mentioned anyone else visiting since he returned from a client meeting.

"Who was the client?" Keith asked.

"Mr. Tran," Billie said. "From Rosie's Posies. They swap referrals with Morris's catering company for events."

"You know him, then?"

"We've met. He said he was interested in estate planning, so I recommended my brother."

I recalled the elderly Vietnamese fellow who'd advised me on bouquets for Lydia. He'd inquired once concerning his own wife's mental issues, which were suggestive of dementia, and I'd recommended a specialist.

As for Rafe's peanut allergy, he did his own grocery shopping and read labels carefully, his sister said. He also subscribed to on-line alerts about unlisted allergens in foods.

"How long has he had this allergy?" Keith asked.

"Since we were kids."

"Tell me about that." With more patience than I'd expected, he probed for details of her childhood. Their alcoholic father had abandoned them when she was ten, she related, and their mother had died of heart disease when she was sixteen. Rafe, just out of law school, had saved her from the foster care system by inviting her to stay with him until she turned eighteen.

"He was a father figure?" Keith asked.

"Heavens, no." Billie rolled her eyes. "Our father was verbally abusive. Rafe's completely different."

"How would you describe your relationship?"

"Best friends," she said.

"What happened when you turned eighteen?"

"I started college, worked part-time and moved into an apartment with a couple of other students. I used his place as my permanent address until he got married."

"How did you feel about that?" Keith probed.

"I was glad for him," she said. "Dee Marie was a sweetheart."

"How did she and your brother get along?"

"He adored her," Billie said.

"Ever hit her?"

"Of course not!" Her hands clenched.

"Yell at her?"

"Not around me." Billie seemed to be hanging onto her self-control by a thread. "Is that all?"

"For now." Keith ended with the time. We were rising when Billie said, "I just remembered something."

He switched on his recorder and repeated the information about those present, along with the time lapsed. "What's that?"

Her chest rose and fell rapidly. "Tonight, while Rafe was describing the funeral for me, he drizzled oil on his salad."

"Where'd he get the oil?"

"From his pantry," she said.

"What kind of oil?"

"Olive. Extra virgin, according to the label."

"Does he use that often?" Keith asked.

"Yes. He eats a salad most nights."

"How many people would be aware of that?"

She shrugged. "No idea."

Someone could have contaminated the oil. However, although I'd read that highly refined peanut oil lacks a smell, it also isn't supposed to contain allergens. Only gourmet peanut oils have both.

Again, Keith ended the session. He also withdrew the restrictions on Billie visiting her brother, and she hurried off.

Tory met us in the waiting room, where I took polite leave of Ms. Petrakis. "Thanks for your help."

"Glad to meet you, Dr. Darcy. And you, Ms…"

"Golden." Tory produced a business card. "In case anyone needs a private investigator."

"Thanks." The nurse tucked it into her pocket. "No hard feelings?"

"Not toward you."

Narda's speculative gaze flicked over Keith, but he was too busy reading his text messages to notice. As she started off, he said, "Nurse, would you notify me when Mr. Tibbets wakes up?"

She licked her lips. "All right, detective."

He strode toward the exit. People to see, places to toss. Rafe's house and Morris's catering kitchen, for starters.

When Tory and I reached the walkway, she said, "Too bad he's tied up. Nurse Petrakis seems eager for a rematch."

If Keith was to be believed, he regretted his fling. However, I couldn't vouch for that.

As we approached the parking structure, I asked, "Are you sorry you left the force?"

"Why do you ask?"

"I'm finding you tough to read," I admitted.

"Or you stopped assuming you could read me... Never mind."

Had I assumed that? "Finish the thought."

Backlighting from a security lamp emphasized the heart shape of her face and the softly curling hair. It must drive Keith crazy, this feminine appearance contrasting with the steely interior. Or was it driving me crazy? "I'm not Lydia's kid sister any more."

Neither of us is Lydia's anything. That thought scraped a nerve. Changing direction, I said, "You were a talented police detective. I've been wondering if the private sector lives up to your expectations."

"It's getting there. End of discussion."

"Okay."

Silence reigned until we got in my car. "I just texted Doreen," Tory said. "I'd like to stop by her place to update her. Okay with you?"

It definitely was.

*

When the bell rang at the condo, two sets of footsteps slapped the hall floor. Doreen, her forehead still bandaged, ushered us inside, with Heather fluttering behind her. Both had changed from somber dress clothes into jeans and T-shirts.

"I wish we'd invited people over after the funeral." Doreen gestured us into the sunken living room. "I miss my sister. And judging by who was absent, we'd know who tried to kill Rafe." She clearly believed, like the rest of us, that his collapse had resulted from deliberate actions.

"How is he?" Her girlfriend twisted a strand of pale hair around her finger. "He'll recover, won't he?"

We told them what we'd learned. Our bland surroundings reminded me of the family waiting room at Heights, except that this time, we were the ones answering the questions.

"I guess he didn't throw the cement at me." Shoeless, Doreen tucked her feet beneath her on the couch. "But if he's innocent, who's doing this?"

"The caterer," Heather blurted from beside her. Either she didn't realize or didn't care that she was speaking of Tory's father. "Or his assistant. She delivered food for your mom right before she died, too."

"Mom was already dead when they got there," Doreen told her.

"So that girl claims!"

"Calm down." Doreen patted her shoulder.

"I can't!" Heather cried. "Whatever poisoned Rafe, it had to be in the food."

"He did sprinkle oil on his salad, from his pantry," I said.

Tory dropped me a shut-the-hell-up look. She was right. I'd just disclosed evidence unnecessarily.

"Have they searched his house?" Heather said. "Surely there are fingerprints or DNA."

Doreen frowned. "Why don't you have a drink? You're really on edge."

"Sure I'm on edge," Heather snapped. "Rafe's lying in the hospital fighting for his life."

"I had the impression there was no love lost between you," Tory said.

"That doesn't mean I wished him harm." Rising, Heather began to pace.

I'd grown suspicious of her over-the-top reaction. "What aren't you telling us?"

"It's the money." The words flew out, unguarded.

"What do you mean, the money?" Doreen's face flushed almost as red as her hair. "You mean Mom's? Did you cheat her?"

As executor, Rafe had been investigating the financials. Some of Malerie's losses dated from before her consultation with Heather, but there'd been a big one more recently. And he'd threatened in front of everyone to identify the source.

"No! Yes. Not intentionally." Without her high heels, Heather in motion was barely taller than the rest of us, seated. "When we discussed her estate, she asked if I could recommend any hot investments."

"Did you?" Tory asked.

"I was excited about this diagnostics company I'd heard of through friends," Heather said. "Since I bought into it, my money had doubled, and I believed it might be about to double again."

"Did these friends work for the company?" Tory asked. "Did they describe a product that hadn't been released?"

The guilt on Heather's face betrayed the answer. Insider trading—buying or selling stocks or securities based on confidential information—is illegal.

"I was trying to assist Mrs. Abernathy, not hurt her," she said. Which didn't answer the question.

"You're the reason she went broke." Anger tightened Doreen's features.

Heather's voice shook. "Not on purpose."

"Tell me the rest. All of it."

"A month later, I learned there were problems, that they'd lost key employees and their R&D was behind schedule," Heather said. "It was simple prudence to sell my shares."

"Without telling Mom." In her fierce concentration, Doreen ignored Tory and me.

"I had no idea she'd acted on my tip, let alone invested heavily," Heather said. "You have to believe me."

"How much did you rake in?" her girlfriend pressed.

"I invested a hundred K and tripled it."

"Two hundred thou in profit. Roughly the same amount Mom lost on that fiasco."

Tears brimmed in Heather's eyes. "I'll do whatever I can to fix this."

Doreen was nearly weeping with rage. "If I hadn't hired a detective, if she and Dr. Darcy hadn't come here tonight, would you have told me?"

"I don't know," Heather admitted.

"What else have you lied about?"

"I never lied about this."

"Sins of omission," Doreen said as if batting away a fly. "You tried to manipulate me into marrying you when you believed I was an heiress. Since that didn't work, you got Mom's money another way."

"That's not true!" If Heather gestured any more rapidly, she'd generate enough lift to rise into the air.

"Did you kill her and Rafe to keep it secret?"

"What?" The agitated movements halted. "Of course not!"

"Did you throw that concrete at me?" Doreen shrilled.

"Never!" Heather flung herself toward Doreen. Tory and I leaped up to intervene, but she wasn't on the attack. Instead, she dropped to her knees. "People dismiss me because I'm short and blonde and gay. I've had to fight for everything. I never learned to be frank and open, but I swear I didn't do this on purpose. I'll give you and your sister the money. Every penny."

Doreen slid away. "How can you expect me to trust you again?"

"I promise, I didn't..."

"Get out." Doreen broke off. "Oh, hell, it's her condo. I'm leaving. Tonight."

"No, please. I screwed up, but..." Repeated jabs of the doorbell cut off Heather's words. "Who's that?"

"I'll go see." As if eager to escape her girlfriend's pleading, Doreen stalked up the two steps toward the hall.

I heard the door open and a familiar male voice demand, "Is Heather Blythe here?"

"Yes, detective."

A hard-faced Keith appeared above us in the entry. "Ms. Blythe, I'd like you to accompany me to the station. Now."

"Why?" Trembling, Heather clasped her hands together.

"Rafe Tibbets just woke up. And the last person he recalls seeing at his house was you."

CHAPTER SEVENTEEN

Tory rode with Doreen to the police station to keep tabs on Heather. I returned to the hospital to support Billie and Rafe.

He remained in intensive care. I didn't attempt to intrude, since at this hospital I was a guest. Instead, I located Billie in the small waiting room, which we had to ourselves.

She explained that her brother had awakened shortly after we left. Keith had returned and learned of Heather's visit, but tried in vain to draw out more details. Rafe was too groggy to access the mystery file on the laptop Keith had brought.

"I wish I could do something." Dark circles underscored Billie's gray eyes. "He's always been there for me. We have this special bond."

"Brother and sister." When I was little, I'd longed for a sibling. While my parents hadn't discussed the situation with me, I'd gathered there were fertility issues. Maybe that was part of the reason this field appealed to me. Also, despite an initial interest in psychiatry, I'd fallen in love with babies during my initial rotation in obstetrics.

"We were adopted." The thin young woman fingered a dangling earring. "In a funny way, that drew us closer. Like however bad it got, at least we didn't carry genetic material from those slobs."

"You were both adopted?" I didn't recall her or Rafe mentioning that before.

"Yes."

"Same parents?"

"No."

"Did either of you trace your birth parents?" I inquired more from curiosity than any belief in a link to this case.

Billie shook her purple hair. "I figured if they threw us away once, they'd just reject us again."

"Parents who relinquish babies aren't necessarily throwing them away," I pointed out. "Often they're seeking a better life for their child."

"My mother dumped me at a fire station when I was a day old. She had no interest in finding the right family for me," she said.

"Maybe she was young and scared." I stopped there. Billie had a right to her anger. "What about Rafe?"

"He had birth defects. His parents couldn't be bothered."

Kids with medical issues aren't easy to place. "It's lucky your adoptive parents took him in."

"Oh, they were fostering initially. They got paid extra for him." She took a swig from a can of iced tea.

I've seen foster parents who have a vocation for loving and nurturing children, but there are bad apples. No wonder Rafe and Billie had relied on each other. I wondered how Dee Marie had fit into their relationship.

After a tap on the door, we were joined by an African-American woman, her short black hair salted with gray above her white coat. "I'm Phylicia Berman, the neurologist," she said. "Miss Tibbets?" They shook hands.

"Eric Darcy," I said. "Friend of the family."

"He's a doctor, too," Billie put in.

"OB," I said.

"I see." Most likely the nurse had provided that information already.

"Is my brother all right?" Billie asked.

"The prognosis is hopeful, but head injuries can be tricky." Dr. Berman had a straightforward manner that some patients would find reassuring and others abrasive. As a scientist, I prefer to get my information straight. "Mr. Tibbets is in general good health, which is a plus. The fact that he awoke and was aware of his surroundings is also positive."

"What did the CT scan show?" I asked.

"Brain bruising. No skull fracture or major bleeding." She glanced at her tablet. "Based on his responsiveness, his injury appears mild. However, any trauma to the brain can have residual effects such as headaches, dizziness and irritability."

Irritability? Based on my acquaintance with Rafe, I wasn't sure how we'd tell the difference. But overall, this was good news.

"Was he unconscious from his allergic reaction or from hitting his head?" As an afterthought, Billie blurted, "Or from the shot I gave him?"

"Epinephrine's side effects can include chest pain, fainting and seizures, but that's uncommon," the neurologist said. "Has he used an EpiPen before?"

"Yes. There weren't any problems I'm aware of."

Dr. Berman jotted a note. "Most likely, he lost consciousness due to hitting his head on the floor."

"What's the next step?" I asked.

"Since surgery isn't indicated, the best course of action is to monitor him closely. There's always a risk of a blood clot forming. And it's of prime importance that he rest while his brain heals. Even after he goes home, another blow to the head before he's completely recovered can have severe consequences, possibly fatal."

"Will he remember what happened? Right before he collapsed, I mean," Billie said worriedly.

"We can't be sure." The doctor employed the first person plural, I noticed. Some cynics accuse doctors of brandishing the royal "we" like kings issuing edicts, but in fairness, the neurologist represented a medical team, not only herself. "When patients lose memories immediately prior to an injury, we call that retrograde amnesia. It can last anywhere from minutes to years. In some cases, memory of those events may never return."

"We might not learn who did this?" Billie said. "In any case, it's my fault."

"Why do you say that?"

She shoved her hands into her jeans pockets. "I heard Detective Sparks on the phone with a CSI person. They smelled peanuts in the olive oil jar. Rafe poured it on his food right in front of me. If I hadn't distracted him with my jabbering, he'd have smelled it, too."

Dr. Berman studied her sympathetically. "Loved ones often blame themselves, but that's misplaced. I understand you administered the injection."

"Yeah."

"Then you probably saved his life."

"I guess."

As they talked, I weighed the implications of the oil substitution, which to me erased any doubt that someone had tried to murder Rafe. It was sheer luck that the sound of his fall had alerted his sister. Whoever did it had been sophisticated enough to use a gourmet peanut oil that contained allergens, and familiar enough with his habits to count on him consuming the oil promptly.

The would-be killer had entered the house unobserved. As with Dee Marie's death, that pointed to a family member who had come into possession of both a key and the alarm code. I figured that, like most people, Rafe rarely changed the numbers.

Billie fit that description. But there must be others.

The neurologist departed. Unappeased, Billie scuffed the toe of her jogging shoe against the floor. "I let him down. I should have smelled peanuts."

"Let's focus on the future." No sense harping on blame. "Rafe will be depending on you once he's released from the hospital. Can you stay with him?"

"Sure," she said. "If I don't screw that up, too."

I had no magic potion for repairing self-esteem. However, before leaving, I double-checked to be sure Billie was allowed to sit by her brother's bed.

"I'll call you if he remembers anything else," she said.

"Will you please notify Detective Sparks first?" I requested. "I don't want to step on his toes."

"I get that," Billie said. "Okay."

Wearily, I drove home. Morris had gone to bed, and Tory arrived a few minutes later. Doreen and Heather had dropped her off, she explained over a beer at the counter.

"Keith didn't arrest her?" Being the last person seen by the victim didn't prove guilt, but it was highly suspicious.

Tory plopped her stocking feet on an empty stool. "She swears she went there to tell him about the investment, since she expected that, as executor, he'd discover it anyway. They talked on the porch, according to Heather."

"What about the file? Could she have accessed it?"

"Rafe's computer was turned off when the crime scene team arrived, and it's password protected. And I don't see how anything it contained would threaten Heather. The diagnostics investment didn't happen until months after Dee Marie's death."

"Unless Heather and Malerie had a prior acquaintance."

"Could be. But when Malerie decided to consult an attorney about her will, she asked Doreen's opinion of her roommate. If she already knew Heather, why bother?"

Mentally, I reviewed factors that might have sent Heather on a killing spree. There was the old antagonism between her and Rafe, and the possibility that Dee Marie might have threatened to reveal Heather and Doreen's relationship to her mother. Neither struck me as strong enough motives, but people are unpredictable. Plus, a lot of money had gone missing, more than the few hundred thousand Heather had accounted for.

"How's Doreen taking this?" I asked as I finished my bottle of ale. "Still planning to move out?"

"She's put that on hold," Tory said. "Heather's shaken up. Even if she isn't charged with attempted murder, she's admitted to insider trading. That could get her disbarred. For the present, Doreen's standing by her woman."

"You don't run out on people when they need you," I summarized.

"Not if you're a decent human being," she agreed.

After an exchange of goodnights, it was off to bed. I slept heavily and awoke late, unusual for me. The Sunday paper produced a stunner: Soraya Montenegro's article, headlined "Mother-Daughter Slayer Sought," was accompanied by a photo of the funeral, with Rafe, Tory and me in the foreground. Only Rafe was identified, with Tory and me described simply as mourners.

The article mentioned his hospitalization as well as Doreen's close encounter with a chunk of concrete. The reporter was thorough and the writing professional, if unwelcome.

While my work involves life and death issues, it takes place in private. With this exposure of Malerie's family, the newspaper had ripped a wall out of their homes and invited in the public. They'd become unwilling participants in a reality show.

Keith might be facing camera crews this morning. I hoped that wouldn't pressure him into arresting anyone prematurely.

As it turned out, Billie phoned an hour later, having already called the detective. "My brother's more alert," she said in the hoarse tone of someone who's barely slept. "According to him, Heather never entered the house. They just spoke on the porch."

That confirmed her account. The only downside was that we were no closer than ever to identifying the culprit.

*

Sunday afternoon, the police released Morris's catering facility. He hired Sandy to help him clean up. Although he had no scheduled meal service that night, he was determined to resume deliveries on Monday.

At Heights, Rafe drifted in and out of consciousness. A police officer stood by, with Billie in constant attendance. Meanwhile, my hospital summoned me to assist with a multiple birth.

Another patient arrived with premature labor, a month and a half early at thirty-four weeks. I prescribed medication to halt the contractions. As long as I was on hand, I also performed a C-section on a woman in labor whose baby was showing signs of distress.

By the time I finished, dusk was falling. Since there'd be no Morris at my house tonight, I drove to the Sea Star Café for dinner.

Located alongside the marina, the restaurant attracts

mostly a lunch crowd, and only a handful of customers occupied tables at this hour. I had my choice of booths to enjoy my pita sandwich and hot chai, a beverage brewed with black tea, cinnamon, ginger and cardamom.

Through the window, I gazed at the peaceful body of water from which the town of Safe Harbor takes its name. It's strictly for pleasure craft, from sailboats to yachts. On a summer day, sails dot the water and the wharf bustles with visitors. Music blares from parties on boats, while shops on the landward side sell surfboards, bait and tackle, bikinis and souvenirs. Tonight, the stores were shuttered and only a few boats drifted toward their moorings.

The indoor lights reflected in the glass, and with my vision obscured, I didn't pay much attention to a woman hurrying along the pier, hugging herself against the breeze. Returning from a sail, presumably, and eager for the warmth of her car.

A streetlight caught the unusual red of her hair. Was I imagining the color? Then I glimpsed a face so familiar my breath caught.

She was too thin for Doreen; it must be Danielle. But thinner than Danielle, too, and with hair cropped short.

Take a picture, you idiot. I fumbled with my phone. At this distance and angle, it recorded only a tiny image obscured by reflections. Leaving the remains of my meal, I raced past other diners onto the wharf.

Nobody there.

Speeding up the steps to the parking area, I still found no one. Damn damn damn.

I listened for an engine. On the street, a car rattled off, its taillights vanishing as I reached the curb. Someone must have picked her up.

I lingered, staring about in case that hadn't been her ride, but nothing stirred. Retracing my steps, I tried to figure out which boat she'd come from. If she'd gone sailing or attended an on-board party, perhaps I'd spot someone else, but I didn't.

My heart thumped in my ears. When I checked my picture, it revealed—as I'd feared—little more than a blur. However, I have excellent eyesight and I knew what I'd seen.

Malerie's so-called quadruplet was real.

CHAPTER EIGHTEEN

Knowing something and proving it—or persuading others that it's true—are different matters. Especially if those others are annoyingly determined to use logic and stick to verifiable evidence.

"This could be the abominable snowman or D.B. Cooper." Keith, who'd been killing a few beers with Tory at my kitchen table, squinted at the image I'd forwarded to his phone.

"I saw her," I said. "She's the spitting image of Malerie's daughters." Except for the short hair, but that could have been a wig.

"There's a theory that everyone has a doppelganger." After a futile attempt to enlarge the image to reveal detail, Tory wrinkled her nose and set her phone aside. "Also, it was late, it was getting dark and you want to believe, like Fox Mulder on *The X-Files*."

"This isn't an extraterrestrial. And Malerie saw her too." The argument sounded weak even to me. I was no closer to establishing the woman's existence than before I glimpsed her.

"Any chance she's a forensic accountant?" Keith asked. "I could use one."

"Why?"

"As I'm sure you've already heard, Mrs. Abernathy's records are a tangle."

Tory chimed in. "We haven't been able to gain full access yet, but Rafe's raised a lot of questions."

Did "we" refer to her and Doreen or her and Keith? Or was the royal "we" again raising its likely-to-be-guillotined head?

In the fridge, I compared the merits of alcoholic beverages and fruit juice or some combination thereof. Considering my low level of credibility tonight, I stuck to a cranberry-apple blend.

"What about Rafe's mystery file?" I pulled up a chair. "Has that shed any light?"

"He refuses to retrieve it until he's in better shape." Keith ran a hand through his dark-blond mop. If it got any messier, one of Lydia's beloved hummingbirds might build a nest in it.

"He's afraid we'll go Dumpster-diving through his client records," Tory explained.

"I assured him that at this point a judge would give us a subpoena, and he told me to go ahead and try." With his forearm, Keith wiped a beer ring from the table. "Typical lawyer."

"The guy wakes up from a coma spouting disclaimers," she elaborated.

They were tagging onto each other's sentences, like in the old days. I remained wary. Their truce didn't preclude a bomb detonating without warning.

Keith took another swallow. "We need to examine the payees' records. I wish Morris... Sorry. Loose tongues and all that."

Tory narrowed her eyes at him. "You don't mean you suspect Dad."

He shrugged.

"As if my father had anything to do with this, other than by pure chance." My sister-in-law turned to me. "From what Rafe says, Mrs. Abernathy paid her bills haphazardly. There were overpayments to some creditors, including Dad."

"Big overpayments," Keith muttered.

"And underpayments, too. Dad claims it balanced out."

"Funny way to run a business," Keith said.

"He hates to hassle clients." Tory spoke fondly.

"Which is why he nearly went bankrupt a few years ago, right?" said her ex-boyfriend. I was with Keith on this one. Morris's soft heart made him easy prey for deadbeats.

She ignored the remark. "There were also large donations to the animal shelter, most of which Ilsa Ivy claims she didn't receive."

"If her bookkeeping is as unconventional as her funeral eulogies, that proves zilch." Keith stretched his legs, bumping me. "Am I bothering you, doll?"

"It's fine, sweetie," I answered.

"Oh, hell." He withdrew his feet.

When the conversation drifted to the football season, I headed upstairs. Tomorrow, with Rafe gaining strength and the banks open for business, there was a good chance of more discoveries on the financial front. But as for unearthing information about Malerie's alleged quadruplet, I'd have to do it myself.

*

The normalcy of my office on a Monday morning restored my equilibrium: Glenda beaming from the reception desk, Farrah juggling appointment cancellations and requests; a couple of early-arriving patients staring at their phones in the waiting room—my world felt on track.

Except for the fact that I'd encountered a woman who challenged the fabric of reality. While that might be an exaggeration, there was a lumpy knot of yarn snarling the smooth weave. Who was she, how was she related to the Abernathy triplets, and why didn't she show up in our records?

Whenever I had a spare minute, I dug through my office on the chance that Malerie's old file might be stuffed in a drawer or wedged behind shelved books where my earlier searches had missed it. No luck. Finally, although not eager to reveal myself as a kook, I related yesterday's sighting to my partner.

Buttonholed in the break room, Isaiah sipped his coffee as he listened. "Sorry for not getting back to you about Mrs. Abernathy," he said when I'd finished. "I did remember something."

"What's that?"

"Her file indicated she was a multipara." The older doctor spoke as casually as if discussing his latest golf score. "Does that help?"

The world tilted sideways. "Yes."

A pregnant woman is termed a primigravida during her first pregnancy and a multigravida or multipara during the second. Malerie had given birth prior to the triplets.

In retrospect, that should have been obvious, except why hadn't she raised the matter herself? If she'd had a baby and relinquished it for adoption, surely that explanation should have struck her as soon as she spotted the woman on the bus.

She'd said that people lie. Who? And how could someone have told a lie so big, so devastating, that it was worth killing to cover it up?

Isaiah went off to see patients, and I tended to mine. I refused to allow the subject into my conscious mind until midday, when I received a call from my housekeeper.

"I'm sorry to bother you, Dr. Darcy." On the phone, Sandy had a slightly nasal voice. "I'm at your house and I wondered if you'd be home for lunch. I'm worried about Morris and it would be easier to discuss it in person."

"What about Morris?" Then it hit me: if anyone knew Malerie's secrets, it was her old friend. Since a nurse's aide or a good housekeeper is discreet, I could hardly blame Sandy if she'd withheld sensitive information, especially since it dated from decades ago and bore no obvious relationship to recent events. "Actually, I will drop by. I can't stay long."

"I'll have a sandwich waiting for you," she said.

"It's not necessary."

"Glad to do it."

I dislike taking advantage of an employee. "Thanks, but I prefer to buy one. See you in a few minutes."

At home, I found a note saying Sandy was upstairs cleaning the master bathroom. To save time, I carried my sandwich with me.

When I reached the steps, a trace of Lydia's perfume reminded me of the conservatory off to my right. Tory's searching had failed to discover any sign of the stolen jewelry on the Internet or locally. I hated whoever had taken it. How irrational, when the burglar might also be a murderer and deserved far more condemnation on that score. However, this loss felt intensely personal.

On the second floor, I passed the exercise room which, true to her word, Tory had stopped using. I'd emailed her permission to work out any time other than early mornings, but she'd stuck to her resolve.

This brought me to the master bathroom. Before Lydia remodeled, it had featured an outdated expanse of tan tile with brown grout, walls painted maroon, and a wooden toilet seat that forty years ago must have been à la mode, or à la commode. For my mother, who'd suffered recurring bouts of chemotherapy, this had been both a refuge and a torture chamber where nausea reigned.

My wife had transformed it with a skylight, soothing colors

and updated fixtures. Dad's favorite change, and mine after Lydia and I inherited the master suite, was the installation of a separate shower and a large, open tub deep enough for a thorough soak.

When I entered, my housekeeper, blond hair tucked under a scarf, was on her knees in the tub, rubbing with a non-abrasive cleanser. I stepped over the cord attached to my hand vacuum and sat on the padded stool at the dressing table.

"Take a break," I said. "I'll pay for your extra time."

Sandy responded with a smile. "Thanks, but I promised to assist Morris later with the cooking and deliveries. Besides, I'm more comfortable keeping busy."

"I understand." Although the stool cramped my legs, I considered how much more uncomfortable Sandy must be. "What's bothering you about Morris?"

"He's very tense. I think he feels guilty about what Billie's been through." She frowned at a spot on the tub. "He's also disturbed about his bookkeeping."

"I heard Mrs. Abernathy's payments were haphazard," I said.

"He's convinced the police suspect him of stealing from her." Sandy sprayed the spot and took a few swipes.

"He would never do that." I spoke around a mouthful of food.

"Of course not. Would it be unethical for you to ask Detective Sparks to go easy on him?"

"Probably not but it might look suspicious." Anyway, Tory was already springing to her father's defense.

"Well, I fear for his health. He's sixty-two, on the chubby side and he doesn't exercise." Sandy surveyed the tub again. "And as far as I can tell, he avoids doctors. Professionally, I mean."

"I'm afraid so." The old saying about the shoemaker's

children going barefoot applies to doctors' families too. My mother had sworn by her organic diet and refused to get a mammogram until too late. I'd insisted on regular checkups for Lydia, although for ethical reasons I couldn't treat her myself.

Regarding Morris, I shared Sandy's unease. "My father died of a heart attack at about the same age."

"I didn't mean to upset you, doctor." She began running water, muttering to herself, "This could use a good rinse."

As I finished the sandwich, I recalled my mission. "I hope it's all right if I pose a few questions about Mrs. Abernathy."

"No problem."

My gaze flicked to the wall clock. Was it really that late? I cut to the point. "She had a baby before the triplets, didn't she?"

Sandy sighed. "I should have told you, but I hated to bring up such an ugly business."

"What was ugly about it?"

She rested on the broad lip of the tub, bare feet in the water. "When I left, Mal was pregnant with Winston's baby. She bragged that he'd leave his barren wife for her, which I thought was both immoral and cruel."

"You weren't here when she delivered?"

Sandy shook her head. "I'm not clear on the details, except that the baby was born with heart defects."

A memory slotted into place: Danielle citing her mother's regrets about smoking and its effects on Dee Marie's asthma. There'd been a reference to heart damage, which I'd assumed referred to Winston's death. But she must have meant this baby.

"A girl, right?" That would explain the mystery woman.

"I'm not sure. Mal referred to her child as `it.'" Sandy shuddered. "She couldn't bear to hold the poor little thing. I was horrified."

"What happened to... it?"

"It died." She swallowed.

That explained why Malerie didn't suspect she had another child running around. "Who told you that?"

"She did," Sandy said. "There wasn't even a funeral. Winston was in such a hurry to hush it up before his wife found out that he rushed the burial arrangements."

People lie. Was it possible Winston had put up the baby for adoption without Malerie's knowledge? Despite legal obstacles, a wealthy doctor presumably had connections.

"Was that when they broke it off?" I asked.

She nodded. "He dumped her, to put it plain. For years, she avoided any mention of him."

"Until his wife died?"

"And he landed in the hospital, where she was on his medical team." Sandy peered down at her clasped hands. "I should have been frank with you, doctor, but it would have put Mal in a bad light and hurt her daughters. There's been enough harm done to this family."

"I saw her," I blurted.

Sandy gave a start. She didn't seem to notice the water sloshing around her ankles. "Who?"

"A red-haired woman nearly identical to the triplets," I said. "Except her hair's cut short."

"Where?"

"At the harbor."

"My goodness!" She rose abruptly. "Oh, heavens, look at the water I'm wasting." Pivoting, she reached for the faucet, slipped and reached out for support.

I lunged to catch her. Although I'm not normally clumsy, the movement threw me off balance and at the same instant, Sandy shifted her weight unexpectedly. While I plunged forward, she tumbled sideways, clutching at the vacuum cord. The small appliance flew through the air.

I thrust a hand into the tub to break my fall. A splash hit my face as the vac landed and, at the same instant, I registered the click of the ground fault interrupter Lydia had installed in the electrical outlet. The device can be annoyingly overactive, shutting down my razor for no apparent reason, but it had just saved my life, or at least spared me a bad shock.

"Damn. That was close." I shut off the faucet, opened the drain and hauled myself out. "Are you all right?"

Sandy lay on the tile, breathing hard. "I... Yes. How about you?"

"I'm fine. I wish I could say the same for my clothes." At the sink, I unplugged the vacuum and hit the GFI reset button. Vivien had recommended a hand vac with a cord because it's more powerful than the battery type, but from now on, it was banned from the bathroom. "I have to change. Take the rest of the afternoon off, with full pay. Honestly, I don't know how that happened."

"Tubs are slippery." After stashing the cleaning supplies in a plastic carrier, Sandy hurried out.

We could both have been electrocuted, I reflected as I put on dry clothes. But why had an experienced housekeeper placed a plugged-in appliance close to a water source?

My cell rang, interrupting my train of thought. "Tory?"

"I'm at the hospital." She sounded breathless.

"What's wrong?"

"It's Rafe. One minute he was sitting up, talking to us. And then... " She stopped.

Hell, no. "He can't be dead."

"They tried to save him." Tory was crying. "They rushed him into surgery but he died in the operating room. The doctor said it was a blood clot."

He'd been on the road to recovery. When Dr. Berman cited

the risk of a pulmonary embolism, I'd discounted it.

"How's Billie?" I asked.

"That's the funny thing, Eric." Tory cleared her throat. "She's disappeared."

CHAPTER NINETEEN

Billie hadn't exactly vanished, I learned from Tory. She'd packed up her car and lit out for places unknown.

Billie had been with her brother all morning. If anyone could have messed with his IV, it seemed likely to be her, Tory said. Despite no immediate indication of foul play, the autopsy might reveal more.

I didn't believe Billie had harmed Rafe. Why would she? But then, what was the motive for any of the murders?

Before Tory clicked off, I explained what I'd learned about Malerie's having delivered a previous child. While she didn't seem impressed by the relevance, my sister-in-law promised to share that fact with Keith.

As for the file on Rafe's laptop, Tory said, the police were likely to gain access to that shortly. If the notes belonged to Dee Marie, perhaps they contained references to Malerie's earlier pregnancy.

My mind returned to the question of why Billie had fled and what could have caused her to harm her brother, if she had. What did Malerie's shameful secret, the out-of-wedlock baby apparently abandoned to Winston for disposal, have to do with her?

Billie had told me she was adopted. But she was in her early twenties, younger than the triplets. Malerie's first baby would be in her early thirties.

About the same age as Rafe. And he'd been adopted too.

On the short drive to my office, I conjectured like mad. Assembling puzzle pieces, or ramming square pegs into round holes. Hard to tell which.

Temporarily disregarding the redhead Malerie and I had seen, suppose the baby in question was Rafe? According to his sister, he'd suffered from a birth defect, so that part fit.

From Dee Marie's delving into her mother's papers, he might have begun to suspect his origins. Along with the stunning possibility that he'd married his own sister.

This struck me as straight out of a telenovela. Still, stranger things have happened.

He could hardly have hidden the truth from Dee Marie for long. Then what? Should they reveal what had happened? Divorce? Or carry on and hope nobody found out?

If they'd had a child, there'd have been an elevated risk of birth defects. Everyone carries defective genes, most of which cause no problems because a paired healthy gene compensates. However, receiving such genes from both parents—a risk that increases with a close genetic relationship—can doom a baby to major deformities.

Perhaps they'd argued and it had turned violent. Or Rafe had chosen to escape via a means that preserved his reputation and avoided an expensive divorce, hoping to disguise his wife's murder as an asthma attack.

He'd supposedly been at work when she died. Since his office was within a few miles of home, that didn't preclude his sneaking out. When Malerie summoned her surviving daughters to reveal a big secret, Rafe might have feared it was his birth origin, and killed her.

He might also have roped Billie into the plot. She'd have gone to great lengths to protect her brother. Yet that didn't explain the attack on him.

More speculation: Possibly they'd arranged it to divert suspicion. He'd ingested the allergen on purpose and alerted Billie to run back and administer medication. Impossible to foresee that he'd hit his head, with lethal consequences.

Why mention his wife's file to Tory and me, though, if it contained material he'd killed to keep secret? Also, this scenario failed to account for the redhead at the harbor.

My fertile imagination coughed up an answer. Since Malerie had conceived triplets without fertility treatments, she might have had a genetic tendency toward twinning. Rafe and the mystery woman could be siblings.

I'd stumbled upon a theory, however bizarre, that fit. In the parking garage, I called Keith.

Yes, he confirmed, Tory had told him about Mrs. Abernathy's prior pregnancy. So what?

I unloaded my speculation on him. Speaking it aloud, I realized how preposterous it sounded, and braced for a major squelching.

Instead, Keith said, "We'll test Rafe's DNA to see if he was related to Mrs. Abernathy."

"Great." Leaving matters in his hands, I hurried into the office, where my harassed nurse regarded me with exasperation.

I was an hour late. A peek into the waiting room showed it packed with people, some of them pacing.

"I'm really sorry," I said. "It was a matter of life or death."

"I understand." Farrah knew about the murders of Malerie and Dee Marie. Not only had both been patients, but last night the TV news had trumpeted the mother-daughter murders.

Since it seemed unfair for her to continue facing the wrath of our clients, I went out and apologized directly. Anger mutated to irritation and, in a few cases, disbelief as patients and their husbands listened to a doctor humbling himself.

"Are you a hologram?" one woman asked.

I assured her I was not. For those who preferred to reschedule, I promised to work them in soon. Afterwards, Glenda coordinated by phone with patients who hadn't yet arrived, alerting them to the delay and offering to change their appointments.

"You see why I love you?" Farrah murmured as she handed over a face sheet.

"Same here. I'd be lost without you." She's what I've heard described as an office wife. Lydia didn't mind our mutual admiration society, because she knew I never felt any sparks for my nurse. Just great appreciation.

My determination to focus on patients pushed other considerations to the back of my mind. The hours flew by until I received a call from Tory.

"Doreen and Heather are hosting a memorial gathering for Rafe tonight at their condo," she told me. "They believe the family needs to come together. You'll be there, right?"

"What time?"

"Six o'clock," she said. "Dad's catering sandwiches."

I decided against sharing my ideas about Rafe. Until and unless Keith found proof, the man deserved to be mourned. "Have you told your client about her mother's previous pregnancy?"

"Yes, and she's flummoxed." The unevenness in her tone indicated my sister-in-law was walking as she spoke. "It's hard for them to take all this in, as you can imagine."

These days, I could imagine almost anything, I mused. "What about Heather? I doubt she wished Rafe dead, but she was far from his biggest fan."

"According to Doreen, that's changed," Tory said. "When Heather confessed to him about the investment, Rafe accepted her apology and offered to work out some form of reparation to the family."

"That was decent of him," I said.

"Danielle and Fred will be there," Tory added.

"Any others?"

"You and me. I'm not sure who else."

We were all gathering. Unreasoning dread lumped in my stomach. We'd be easy prey, and the killer was still on the loose.

"Keep your guard up," I said. "I have a premonition we'll be in danger."

"Getting superstitious in your old age?"

"Aren't cops supposed to trust their guts?"

"You're not a cop."

"Speaking of police, will Keith be there?" I'd find his presence reassuring.

"It's strictly private, and I doubt Doreen invited him. Anyway, he has more important stuff to do."

Good point. "See you there."

We clicked off. I decided to bring a syringe with a sedative in case anyone went ballistic. Not very practical, since the dose might be inadequate and my chances of getting close enough to jab someone were small, but I needed to feel prepared.

Despite the reshuffling of appointments, I was still seeing patients at six o'clock. My uneasiness mounted. I ought to be at Doreen's.

While I didn't doubt Tory's ability to defend herself, she didn't carry a gun. Speaking of guns, what had happened to Rafe's? I didn't recall Keith saying he'd recovered it.

It was another quarter of an hour before I finished. After a round of apologies to the staff, I departed at a rapid clip, the syringe tucked into my tote bag.

And ran right into Jeremiah, waiting by the elevator. He greeted me with, "Eric. I did not see you at lunch."

"I ate at home." I peered at the position indicator over the doors. One car was on the ground floor, the other a couple of stories above us on the sixth.

"I owe you my thanks."

"For what?" Neither elevator moved.

"Your advice." Jeremiah shifted his lanky frame. I had the impression that towering over me bothered him. "I am grateful that I did not fire my nurse for arguing with her mother."

Why bring this up now? "Glad she worked out."

"She is excellent," he announced. "Did you not find it difficult to secure a top-quality nurse?"

"I more or less inherited Farrah. Her aunt used to work for Dad." The indicator showed the upper car descending toward us. *Hurry up.*

"I searched for many months," Jeremiah intoned. "How strange that, despite living in such a populous state as California, I had to hire someone from Idaho."

"Idaho?" The elevator whispered to a halt and the doors slid open, revealing an orthopedist whose name I'd forgotten.

"Boise. The name is a corruption of the French word for trees. Did you know that?"

With one foot in the elevator, I halted. Yes, I did, because Sandy had told me.

Sandy, who came from Boise. Sandy, whose involvement with Malerie dated back for decades. Was this a coincidence?

As Keith had said about my missing file, there were way too many coincidences in this case.

"Has your nurse left for the day?" I kept blocking the door. The orthopedist could damn well wait.

"Celia always stays to organize tomorrow's roster." Jeremiah frowned. "Do you not wish to descend?"

At Doreen's condo, the Abernathy clan was gathering. I sensed malevolent forces closing in on them. And on Tory.

Was I yielding to the ridiculous again? A woman who looked just like the triplets, a long-ago baby who might or might not have died, a new nurse from Boise, and a housekeeper also from Boise who'd nearly electrocuted us both only hours ago.

Or rather, who'd nearly electrocuted *me*.

Abandoning the elevator, I grabbed Jeremiah's arm. "Where's your office?"

"This way." To his credit, he didn't object. He's always accepted my actions as meaningful, even when they aren't.

His office lay near the opposite end of the hall from mine. Luckily, no patients lingered in the waiting room to witness me bursting in like a maniac.

Behind the admitting window, a young woman raised her head. Disappointment flooded through me. With long dark hair and Hispanic features, this woman bore zero resemblance to the woman at the harbor.

Making a fool of myself was bad enough, but I'd delayed joining Tory. I also owed Jeremiah an explanation.

"Sorry," I muttered.

"For what?"

The inner door opened. My breath stuck in my lungs as a second woman appeared. "Dr. Schwartz?" said the red-haired nurse. "I thought you'd left."

An off-center smile lit her face. Height, coloring, stance—she could have passed for Danielle or the late Dee Marie.

I'd found the mystery woman. Who the hell was she?

CHAPTER TWENTY

The name tag identified her as Celia Miller. "Is Sandy Miller your mother?" my voice boomed.

A pucker formed between her eyebrows. "Yes. Who're you?"

"This is obstetrician Eric Darcy." Jeremiah radiated pride. "My friend."

"I see." Clearly, she didn't.

For a tangled moment, I had no idea where to begin. *Are you aware your mother is killing people?* Not a brilliant start, especially if Celia was involved. She might whip out a gun, probably Rafe's, and commit an act of workplace violence.

"Were you adopted?" I received quizzical looks from Jeremiah and the receptionist.

"No." After a flicker of hesitation, Celia added, "I don't believe so."

"Were you born with a heart defect?"

"Yes," she said. "What's this about?"

My mother used to say a picture is worth a thousand words. On my phone, I accessed Malerie's Facebook page, where a photo showed her with the triplets.

When I handed it to Celia, she gasped. "Is this

Photoshopped?"

"No. That's your birth mother, Malerie Abernathy," I said. "And those are your younger sisters. They're triplets."

She studied it in amazement. "Do they know about me?"

"The girls don't," I said. "And I'm sorry to tell you that Mrs. Abernathy and one of the triplets have been murdered."

"What?" Pain glimmered in Celia's wide gray eyes. "Who would do that?"

"Your adoptive mother," I said. "Sandy."

Jeremiah brightened. "I saw it on the news last night. The mother-daughter slayings. And that son-in-law is in the hospital."

"He's dead, too."

"I never follow the news," Celia said dully. "I can't believe Mom killed them."

"You'd better start believing it, because if we don't stop her, she'll keep doing it." Or she already was. "Oh, my God."

I fumbled for my phone. After a split second that crawled for an eternity, I pressed my sister-in-law's number. *Pick up pick up pick up.*

"Hey, Eric," said that wonderful voice so much like Lydia's.

"Sandy's the killer," I said. "Has the food arrived? Has anyone eaten?"

"She just dropped it off." At foghorn decibels, Tory yelled, "Don't touch the food! It's poisoned!" Chaos and questions ensued on her end before she addressed me again. "We're okay. You were in the nick of time. What's the deal?"

"I found Malerie's other child," I said. "She's Sandy's adopted daughter and a dead ringer for the triplets. Beyond that, I'm not sure of the story." Or whether Rafe had anything to do with it, and the reason Billie had fled. Even whether the food really had been poisoned, although that was a safe guess. "Did Sandy say where she was headed?"

"No."

"Did your father show up?"

"He was in the van with her but he didn't come in." Behind Tory, Fred's voice demanded an explanation. "I should have listened to you about that quadruplet business. I have to go."

"I'll notify Keith."

"I'll warn Dad," she said. "Stay in touch."

"You bet." The call ended and I pressed my best friend's number. When he answered, I said, "The murderer is Sandy." I told him about Celia.

"That's alarming," he agreed. "But it doesn't prove Mrs. Miller's our suspect."

"She tried to electrocute me today," I said.

"What?"

"Initially, I took it for an accident," I said. "Hand vac in the bathtub. Details later."

"Are you okay?" he demanded.

"Yes."

"Where's Tory? Have you talked to her?"

"She's fine." I described the situation at Doreen's. Then I read him the contents of a text that popped up: *Dad's not answering.*

"Did you lock your house?" Keith asked.

Odd question. "Yes."

"And set the alarm?"

"Of course."

"Did you give Sandy a key or the code?"

"No." Morris had let her in earlier to clean, and she'd left before I did.

"Go home and stay there. Or book a room at a hotel. You're obviously in her sights," he said. "We'll check Morris's premises and her residence."

I didn't recall where Sandy lived. "She has an apartment?"

"Li Tran, the guy from the flower shop, provides a free room in exchange for cleaning his house. Keep me informed."

"Will do." As I clicked off, points of illumination crackled across my brain. As Malerie's nurse/housekeeper, Sandy could have devised a way to copy Dee Marie's and Rafe's key and learn their security code. Also, right after the funeral, she'd overheard him mention the unidentified file. Aware that he had an appointment with her landlord, she'd have felt free to sneak into Rafe's house to contaminate the oil.

"Is Mom okay?" Celia asked.

"Try her number," I said. "We need to bring her in safely." *For everyone's sake.*

On her phone, the nurse tapped the readout and listened before speaking. "Mom? It's me. I'm worried about you. Please call back."

She might have been any daughter concerned about her mother. Based on the alleged quadruplet sighting, I'd been chasing a phantom capable of unlimited evil. Now here she stood, pleasant and normal.

Sandy had struck me as pleasant and normal, too. A pleasant, normal sociopath.

I still hadn't pinned down her motives. Theft of Malerie's money? Revenge, but for what?

If she'd conspired with Winston to steal Malerie's baby and lie about her death, it would have been vital to keep Celia's existence secret. Yet any day, I'd have run into Jeremiah's new nurse. Combine that with my investigation, and I understood why Sandy had wanted me dead. That sandwich she'd offered... damn, I'd had *two* close calls.

"I don't understand what's happening," Celia said.

My thoughts spun. "I'm not sure where to begin."

"Mom never told me I was adopted. Can we start with that?"

"I'd like to hear it, too," Jeremiah said. The receptionist seconded the request.

"Thirty years ago, your mother worked with Mrs. Abernathy." I received a nod, indicating she'd heard this part. "Malerie had an affair with a married man and expected him to leave his wife for her when she got pregnant. Then the child was born with a heart defect."

Understanding touched her quasi-familiar face. "Me."

"I'm not sure how Sandy ended up with you," I noted.

"Mom longed for a child," Celia replied. "She said I was everything to her."

"I'm sure that's true."

Frowning, she continued to work through her suddenly altered life story. "Mom claimed my father abandoned us because of the medical bills. The surgeries were expensive."

"No one provided financial assistance?" I couldn't imagine Sandy accepting such an arrangement, however badly she'd wanted a baby.

"My father paid for the first operation," Celia said. "Then he dropped us."

The receptionist, who'd been following this tale avidly, beat me to the punch. "Why?"

"Mom told different stories. She claimed he was broke and alcoholic. Then she'd get angry about how selfish and rich he was. She was mad at Mrs. Abernathy, too. She mentioned breaking an agreement," Celia said thoughtfully. "When I asked what she meant, she'd snap at me."

If Winston had underwritten the initial surgery, the baby hadn't been stolen. Given the reference to an agreement, it appeared Sandy had adopted the baby with his and Malerie's permission. Then they'd stiffed her. Getting stuck with huge bills for further surgeries and treatments must have fueled Sandy's resentment. If so, it had been a long, slow burn.

Celia yanked me out of my reverie. "Who was my father?"

"Winston Abernathy," I said. "A doctor who practiced here. I knew him slightly."

"He was a distinguished anesthesiologist," Jeremiah added.

Celia hugged herself. "I spun fantasies about my dad showing up and loving me. Instead, he turns out to be a snob. I wasn't perfect enough to be his precious daughter."

How strange to view Winston Abernathy, M.D., respected member of the community, through the eyes of the out-of-wedlock baby he'd apparently cast off. To avoid the scandal and expense of leaving his wife for his mistress? Because he couldn't accept a child with heart problems? Or simply because he was a self-centered jerk?

"Didn't he and Mrs. Abernathy get married, though?" Celia asked. "I mean, obviously, they did. She was using his name."

"They got together after his wife died in a car accident," I said. "You'd have been a toddler by then."

Whenever Malerie and Winston looked at the triplets, they must have seen the face of the baby they'd rejected. Surely there'd been regrets. Had they tried to see her or even reclaim her?

There were a lot of pieces missing. "Why did your mother return to Safe Harbor?"

"About a year ago, she lost her job in Boise," Celia said. "Coincidentally, her old friend had a hip replacement and hired her for in-home care. Mom only planned to stay a few months, but she kept extending it."

Surely none of that would have occurred if Sandy and Malerie were at odds about their daughter. What had Sandy told her old friend—that her daughter had died? It would have been credible.

Once Sandy arrived, she must have seen a chance to siphon off the money she believed was her due. In view of Malerie's careless record-keeping, embezzlement would have been easy until Dee Marie stepped in to straighten out the mess.

Celia's arrival in Safe Harbor had ultimately exposed Sandy's lie. "Surely your mother objected to your moving here," I said.

"She went ballistic," Celia admitted.

"Hence your arguments with her," Jeremiah observed.

"Why'd you come, then?" asked the receptionist.

"We'd always been close. It seemed natural for me to join her," his nurse answered. "I missed her, and I wanted to find out more about my father."

"Didn't she tell you he'd died?" I asked.

"Yes, but Mom fudges the truth when it suits her." Now, there was an understatement. "Like I told you, she couldn't keep the stories straight. She claimed he'd been abusive, like her father, and that I should be grateful he was gone, but the tale kept growing until he practically had horns and a tail. I started to hope she'd invented the whole thing and he might be alive."

"I'm sorry," I said. "Winston died of a stroke four years ago."

"I'll never meet either of my birth parents." Tears darkened Celia's lashes. "I had no idea I was adopted or that I had sisters."

"One of whom Sandy murdered," I said.

"Are you sure?"

"Yes." I no longer had any doubts.

"There might be a reasonable explanation," offered the receptionist, obviously unaware of the extent of Sandy's depravity. Or perhaps she was one of those overly evolved beings whose survival instincts had been bred out of her.

"Mom swore terrible stuff would happen if I searched for my father," Celia murmured. "If I hadn't, would those people still be alive?"

"An interesting conundrum," Jeremiah remarked.

"Your sister Dee Marie was murdered six months ago," I pointed out. "Long before you got here."

"Thank you, Dr. Darcy." Celia wiped her eyes with a tissue. "I'm glad I'm not to blame for that, at least."

"You're not to blame for anything," the receptionist assured her. That part, I agreed with.

"I've kept you all too long." Celia picked up her purse.

"You ride the bus, don't you?" I asked.

"Yes. How did you know?"

"Mrs. Abernathy spotted you. She lost sight of the bus before she could catch up." On impulse, I added, "I'll give you a lift to your place. Where are you staying?"

She named a motel, and accepted the ride. I could be running a risk; her physical resemblance to the Abernathy triplets didn't preclude an inner landscape as dark and twisted as Sandy's. Maybe Celia was part of this plot and played a role in an escape plan.

I doubted that, however. And I had the syringe in my tote, for whatever it was worth.

Jeremiah accompanied us to the parking structure. For once, I didn't mind. In fact, I appreciated having a reinforcement in case we were waylaid.

At the charging station, Celia blinked at the identical cars side by side. "You guys have a twin thing?"

"We possess similar tastes," Jeremiah remarked.

"I guess you do."

She buckled herself into my passenger seat. A minute later, as we rolled down the hospital's drive, she spoke again. "Dr. Schwartz seems fixated on you. What's with that?"

"He's a bit eccentric." Accurate enough.

"He sure is," Celia said. "I like him, though."

That spoke well of her. However, I faced a decision,

whether to proceed inland to her motel or take her home with me. Not that I had designs on Celia. Yet if Sandy contacted anyone, it would be her daughter. We had to catch her before she devised yet another vicious plot.

"Look, I can drop you at your place, but the homicide detective recommended I go home and lock the doors." He'd also mentioned staying at a hotel, but I'd rather not. "You're welcome to join me. There's no telling what your mother will do if she feels cornered."

"She'd never hurt me!"

"She might harm someone else." Would Celia deny that Sandy posed a threat? I wondered.

Slowly, she said, "At your place, I can keep tabs on the investigation better than at the motel, right?"

"Absolutely."

"Okay."

I steered toward the ocean. Beside me, Celia fiddled with her purse. "What if someone's framing her? It's possible."

"I'd agree if I hadn't seen it for myself." I described my near-electrocution in the bathroom. "It was so smooth, it didn't even register with me until later. Or do you think I'm overreacting?"

Celia pressed her lips together before replying. "My mother wouldn't be that careless," she admitted. "She's warned me about unplugging devices before I run the water. Especially anything other than a hair dryer, because they have an automatic shutoff."

As the traffic thinned, I accelerated southward. "By the way, were you at the harbor last night?"

She gave me a startled glance. "Yes. You saw me?"

"I ate dinner at the pier."

"A guy invited me to a party on his boat. Turned out to be a party of just him and me." Celia smiled ruefully. "I high-tailed it out of there."

"I tried to follow, but you disappeared."

"Mom picked me up,"

What if I'd seen Sandy? But, typically, I hadn't. She'd been a presence in the background the past few weeks, at Doreen's condo, at the funeral, at my house. Without my suspecting a thing.

Anger gripped me. She'd violated my home, not once but repeatedly. No doubt it had been Sandy who broke in and stole Malerie's file.

Now that I thought about it, Morris had hired her based on business cards dropped off by would-be cleaners, which meant she'd probably planned the theft in advance but grown impatient. Ironically, if she'd delayed a few more days, we might have employed her as a housekeeper and she'd have been able to steal the file with no one the wiser.

And I wouldn't have lost Lydia's jewelry. What had she done with it?

We traced side streets to where my familiar home welcomed us, dark half-timbers punctuating pale-gray brickwork.

Beside me, Celia sighed. "You live here? It's beautiful."

"Thanks." I parked in the driveway, sparing her the clutter of the garage. "It belonged to my parents."

"It's like being invited into Sleeping Beauty's castle."

"I suppose it is."

Outside, I moved past her up the front walk and unlocked the door. As I swung it open, from the corner of my eye, I recognized a vehicle parked down the street, a white van with gold trim and brown lettering. Despite a palm tree screening the view, it was unmistakably Morris's.

I heard no beep-beep from the alarm. Morris had beaten me home. And left a note on the side table, a printed-out letter signed with his rounded flourish.

This was wrong. When he left a note, he scribbled it by hand.

He'd last been seen in the van with Sandy. "Celia, stay back." I took out my phone to call for help.

"This place is amazing." Oblivious to my anxiety, the nurse gazed upwards at the elevated ceiling. And the curving staircase, where—brief mental disconnect—two people poised at the top in an arrangement that made no sense.

Sandy grimaced at us. At this angle, she appeared misshapen in her black-and-white catering uniform. Beside her, a black apron over his clothes, my dazed father-in-law balanced precariously atop a stool.

The electrical cord wrapped around his neck was fastened to the railing. We'd caught Sandy about to stage another death.

CHAPTER TWENTY-ONE

One wrong move and she'd shove my petrified father-in-law over the rail. Judging by his slack muscle tone, Sandy had drugged him. Funny, fierce, loving Morris, who'd gathered me into his big heart, depended on me to save him.

Trying to cover my movements, I tapped a message to Keith. "Sdy at my hs," and hit Send.

"Let him go," I shouted to my so-called housekeeper. "You can't trick us into believing it's suicide."

Renewing her hold on the shorter man, Sandy licked her lips. She hadn't reacted to Celia's presence, perhaps because the nurse stood behind me.

Behind me. Which meant, blocking my escape. If they'd set a trap, I'd walked right into it.

Inside the tote, I touched the syringe. But it would be impossible to sedate them both.

"He begged me to assist him," Sandy cried. "He can't bear the guilt. Read his note. He stole from Malerie and schemed to kill her. Isn't that right, Morris?"

When she yanked the cord, his terrified eyes begged me to stop her. I had no super powers, nothing to halt her except my wits, which under the circumstances didn't amount to much.

On the plus side, Celia hadn't attacked me yet. As far as I could tell with my peripheral vision, she stood frozen.

Stalling, praying for Keith's hasty intervention, I snatched the paper from the table and scanned the lines. "Morris stole from Mrs. Abernathy and murdered her and Dee Marie and Rafe? You expect me to believe this?"

Sandy ignored the comment. "You shouldn't have brought Danielle. I hate those girls. They grew up rich while my daughter suffered."

The red-haired woman edged around me. "Mom?" came Celia's trembling voice. "What are you doing?"

Shocked silence. After a heartbeat, it yielded to anger. "I told you to stay out of my business," Sandy roared. "Why are you here?"

They didn't appear to be in league. Still, the nurse remained an unknown quantity.

"You should have told me I'm adopted." Celia's words echoed in the hall. "I wouldn't have cared."

"You'd have left me for them."

"No, Mom. Why are you killing people? It's crazy."

Beneath the tense exchange, I heard a scraping noise in the garage. The overhead door hadn't groaned open, and the only person with a key to the side entrance was Tory.

Please don't let her burst in here. She'd be as powerless as me. Worse, any sudden intrusion might cost Morris his life.

Sandy remained riveted on her daughter. "Don't believe whatever Dr. Darcy tells you. He's on their side."

"Whose side? My birth family's?"

"Let me tell you about that *family*," Sandy spat. "They'd have dumped you in a ditch if I hadn't taken you. You weren't perfect enough for Dr. Abernathy and his greedy mistress."

"I agree they should have paid for my medical care," Celia began. "But..."

"You think this is about money?" Sandy boomed. "After they finally got married, they tried to buy me off. A quarter of a million dollars for the baby they'd thrown away. Like I'd sell you!"

"You had a right to refuse," Celia protested. "You adopted me legally, didn't you?"

Had Keith read my message? Where was he? I heard no sirens, just a thump from the rear of the house that no one else seemed to notice.

"Sure, but they had money and lawyers." Sandy barely paused for breath. "When I said you died, they acted like I broke a vase. Oh, gee, too bad."

Morris wobbled on his stool. I had a nightmarish image of my father-in-law tumbling off the landing, only to be jerked short by the cord. At this height, it would be likely to break the spine. Blood pressure would drop to zero almost instantly, with brain death occurring in minutes.

Sometimes a doctor can know too much.

"But why murder them now?" Celia demanded. "It might have been awkward if they learned I was alive, but I'm an adult. What could they do?"

"Take you away." Pain twisted Sandy's square face. "Rich mommy, beautiful sisters. What did I have to fight with? I'm a used-up old woman. Barren, thanks to *my* family. After my stepfather raped me, my mother forced me to get a backroom abortion. I nearly bled to death."

Despite everything I knew about Sandy, my gut twisted at what had been done to her as a young girl. Rage had been bottled up waiting to detonate long before the Abernathys entered the picture.

"That's awful." Celia stared at her. "I knew your parents were abusive, but you never told me about the abortion."

"If I'd admitted having a hysterectomy when I was fourteen,

how would I explain giving birth to you?"

"Oh, Mom, I love you," Celia said raggedly. "There's room in my heart for you and another family. You wouldn't have lost me."

"I told you to stay in Boise," Sandy growled. "This is your fault. And yours, Dr. Darcy, for poking into my business. Now I have a surprise for both of you. They're all dead, everyone you care about. I've poisoned them, including your nosy sister-in-law. Here goes the last of them." Baring her teeth, she tightened her grip on Morris.

"Stop!" Celia screamed.

I raced for the stairs, hopelessly late. Above me, movements blurred. Someone—Tory, very much alive—flashed into view. Pulled Morris from the stool. Shouldered aside the furious Sandy.

With Tory handicapped by the need to shield her father and Sandy obsessed with carrying out her plan, a wrestling match put all three of them in jeopardy. When I reached their level, the writhing bodies frustrated my attempts to tackle Sandy, let alone inject her.

Below, someone smashed open the door. "Police!" Celia shrank aside as Keith raced in.

Sandy launched a desperate leap toward her prey, catapulting from the stool to gain an advantage. Bigger, stronger and better trained, Tory deflected the assault.

There was a surreal moment when Sandy rose above the railing, flailing wildly. With eerie slowness, as if in one of her own staged set-ups, she pitched over it head-first. My brain tried to avert the horror by imagining a gymnastic twist and a cushioned landing on hands and feet. Instead, she hit the floor with a sickening crunch.

With a scream, Celia rushed to her mother. But there was nothing a nurse, or anyone else, could do.

*

The evening passed in a swirl of dislocation and unreality. I strained to absorb the fact that Morris, Tory and I had nearly been murdered, along with the rest of Malerie's family.

How had one woman's rage fomented such devastation? And how had I missed it? I couldn't stop shaking as my brain replayed the terrible scene in my home. At the police station, where we underwent interviews, Keith's steady understanding—remarkably sensitive for my rough-edged friend—helped me pull myself together.

Paramedics transported Morris to the hospital, where he seemed physically okay once the drug cleared from his system. Emotionally, he'd have to work through stages of anger, fear and grief. It didn't ease matters that he had to be photographed and swabbed and otherwise thoroughly checked out for evidence, since police had to build a case even though their prime suspect was dead.

As for Tory's timely arrival, she explained that she'd previously installed GPS in her father's van at his request. She'd tracked it to our block, notified Keith—who was already en route, thanks to my text—and sprung into action after she glimpsed our standoff through a front door pane. Fortunately, the lock was loose on her bedroom window, which she'd reached via a ladder from the garage.

Celia tried to cooperate with detectives, but eventually she collapsed and had to be taken to the hospital to be treated for shock. In the span of a few hours, she'd found and lost a family, along with the mother who'd raised her.

Later that night, Billie phoned from Las Vegas, a four-hour drive away, after seeing a news report. She explained she'd fled because Sandy called to say the police were about to arrest her for her brother's murder. She agreed to return voluntarily.

For the next few nights, since my house remained the scene

of an investigation, I rented hotel rooms for Morris, Tory and me. Gradually, bits and pieces fell into place. Tests showed cyanide in the food at Doreen's condo. Rafe's autopsy confirmed that he'd died of a blood clot that had traveled to his heart, and there'd been no indication of foul play at the hospital. I'd forgotten about the DNA test, which to no one's surprise showed he was unrelated to Malerie.

A search of Sandy's room turned up my stolen jewelry and Mrs. Abernathy's medical file, as well as Dee Marie's laptop and documents. The mystery file on Rafe's cloud did indeed belong to his late wife and included questions about a baby with heart defects, along with a chilling note Dee Marie had written to herself: "Ask Sandy."

Perhaps she'd been trying to spare her mother's sensibilities. If so, her kindness had proved lethal.

Malerie's finances remained to be unraveled, but much became clear. She'd entrusted her old friend with bill paying, and Sandy had seized the opportunity to embezzle. She'd left a jumbled trail of unexplained withdrawals, odd payments and diverted checks aimed at confusing whoever tried to sort things out.

About twenty thousand dollars turned up in an account in Sandy's name. However, the financial damage she'd created was minor compared to the losses from Malerie's bad investments. She'd gambled with her inheritance, and lost.

Heather's promise to pay her gains to Doreen and Danielle was a personal matter. As for the insider trading angle, I considered that none of my business.

One more sad detail involved Sandy's claim that, on the afternoon of Malerie's death, she'd been working for an elderly employer. Under questioning, the client revealed that she suffered from early-stage Alzheimer's, a fact she'd kept hidden. She had no idea whether her housekeeper had left the premises.

Morris, Tory and I moved back into my house on Thursday. It, along with the catering premises, had been scrubbed by a service that specializes in crime scene and biohazards cleaning.

While the sense of violation persisted, I refused to let anyone drive me from the place where I'd grown up and where Lydia and I had lived. It helped to share it with two people who'd endured the same loss, who also awoke from nightmares, who could prop up each other and me.

On Friday, Celia insisted on returning to work for Jeremiah. Aware that she needed to talk and that I needed to listen, I shared a patio table with the two of them.

Like me, Celia regretted not having detected a serious problem sooner. She also wondered, in retrospect, if there'd been a previous murder.

A few years after Sandy's mother succumbed to liver disease, she explained, the abusive stepfather, a diabetic, had died suddenly of what was ruled natural causes. From the bitter satisfaction with which her mother had referred to his demise, Celia believed Sandy might have injected him with an overdose of insulin.

"If she got away with murder once," Celia told us over a taco salad, "she must have figured she could do it again."

"That is logical," Jeremiah concurred.

As for the concrete that hit Doreen's windshield, Celia recalled shopping at a specialty market nearby that day and arguing with her mother. She'd been mad enough to insist on taking the bus home. Most likely, Sandy had feared Doreen would spot the look-alike and had thrown the chunks to distract her.

Having apparently run out of topics, Celia fell silent as she ate. The occasional side glance at me spoke volumes, however. What was she looking for? What was *I* looking for?

If only I had a name for the malaise that had dogged me since Monday's crisis. Dismay, guilt, sorrow—they figured in, but there was more.

Since Malerie's death, I'd been propelled by a mission. It had come as a relief from the remorse of failing to save my wife, or even understand why our marriage had crumbled. I had hoped that exposing the killer would bring a sense of resolution, but it didn't.

"May I ask a favor?" Celia's attention fixed on me. Jeremiah's did the same.

"Of course."

"It's sensitive."

"Try me."

She tilted her head. At this angle, despite the close range, she could easily have passed for Dee Marie. "Would you go with me to Mr. Tibbets's funeral tomorrow?"

Sensitive? Explosive might be more accurate. Malerie's surviving daughters were reeling from a series of blows, including their own near-deaths. Learning that they had an older sister raised by their mother's slayer had disturbed them. According to Tory, Celia's existence added to their heartache by casting mud on their parents' memories.

"Are you sure that's what you want?" I asked. "It could be an unpleasant experience."

"I'm more concerned about upsetting my sisters." Celia's fork mashed the remains of her lunch. "I don't blame them for rejecting me after what Mom did. But it's important to pay my respects."

That was a tough request. I could hardly refuse, though. Besides, I'd already planned to attend. "Will you speak to them?"

"Not if it's awkward." Her shoulders sagged. "I wrote to Danielle and Doreen to express my sympathy and regrets. They haven't answered."

"You should go," Jeremiah said.

Celia regarded him questioningly. "Why do you think so?"

"You are staying on as my nurse, I trust."

"Yes."

"You will encounter them around town," he continued. "They must accept the reality of your living here. And you also have been a victim of injustice. As you do not hold them responsible for their parents' misdeeds, they should extend the same grace to you."

His wisdom impressed me. I regretted, a little, that Jeremiah's irritating qualities had estranged us. Still, I couldn't be around him for long without remembering that he'd once been Lydia's lover.

"Thank you, Dr. Schwartz." Celia reached out as if to cup his folded hands, then thought the better of it. "Dr. Darcy, are you okay with going?"

"Sure. I'll pick you up at your motel," I said.

Danielle and Doreen might never forgive me. That was a risk I was willing to take.

CHAPTER TWENTY-TWO

In the week since Malerie's funeral, November had arrived and the black-and-orange Day of the Dead trappings had departed. A sharp breeze whipped the cemetery, chilling us despite the weak sunshine.

A tearful Billie, her once-purple hair dyed black, hung on Morris's arm as she joined her in-laws in the front row. The other mourners included a few familiar faces, along with a sprinkling of people I didn't recognize. Tory and a security guard held the news media at bay.

At Malerie's funeral, Rafe had been the outsider, lingering on the grass with Tory and me. Today, I stood with Celia at a discreet distance from the family. While Doreen and Danielle hadn't replied to Celia's letters, they hadn't banned her, either. According to Tory, they'd concluded it would cause the least amount of fuss to tolerate her, and counted on me to restrain any unseemly behavior.

I appreciated their faith in me. However, it was hard to imagine this subdued woman, her face half-hidden beneath the brim of a hat, bursting out in an offensive manner.

The man who rose to address the gathering was fortyish, with graying temples and a calm manner. He introduced himself as Rafe's pastor. Unlike Ilsa Ivy, he'd not only come to bury the dead, he intended to praise him.

The pastor cited Rafe's struggles since childhood with neglectful parents, a birth defect—a clubfoot—as well as his devotion to his sister, his wife's asthma and then her murder. He didn't shrink from mentioning the manner of Rafe's death.

"How can those who loved him hope to recover from such a vicious act?" he asked. "Should we forgive the evildoer?"

As always during the past year, whenever the subject of death arose, I thought of Lydia. It would be intolerable if she'd been murdered. I didn't believe I was capable of forgiving anyone who'd harmed her.

"Some people declare that because each of us has sinned, we must forgive our fellow men and women as we would wish for God to forgive us. Others contend that only the victim of a crime has the right to grant absolution, and that is not humanly possible in a murder," the pastor went on.

"Whether to absolve the guilty is a matter for our individual consciences, especially in a case where justice can't be dealt out in a courtroom," he said. "But in order to heal, there is one person we must pardon."

He paused for a dramatic moment, allowing us to speculate about whom he meant, before saying, "That is ourselves. When someone dies, we instinctively relive our sins of omission and commission, our imperfections, the kind words left unspoken and the hurtful words we can't take back. As part of the mourning process, we need to release our guilt. None of us is perfect, nor are we required to be. What we owe the departed is to embrace their memories with joy and to gather our surviving loved ones close."

He seemed to be speaking directly to me. This past year, I had pushed everyone away. I should have been more supportive of Morris and Tory. And perhaps of myself.

After the eulogy, in a shaky voice, Billie read a favorite poem of Rafe's. When she faltered, Danielle finished the poem, then thanked everyone for joining them. As guests got to their feet, she gazed over the green expanse, caught my eye and mouthed the word, "Wait."

Most of the mourners drifted toward the mortuary building. The pamphlet distributed on arrival had invited us to a gathering with refreshments.

Beside me, Celia pushed her purse strap higher on her shoulder. "We should leave."

"Danielle wants us to wait," I said.

"She does?"

"I think so." Had I misread her lips? Maybe she'd said, "What!" Oh, well, we'd find out.

First we had to face a scowling Doreen, who strode across the grass toward us. Heather plunked along in her wake.

Shrinking toward me, Celia bumped her hat against my shoulder. A gust of wind tore it off, and only her fast grab saved it from whipping away.

Doreen halted in astonishment. Breathing fast, Heather caught up, and she too stared at the newcomer.

"You look just like Dee Marie," Doreen exclaimed.

"And Danielle," Heather murmured.

"No, her nose is thinner. Danielle's, I mean. Otherwise they're almost identical."

To me, the creases touching Celia's eyes and mouth marked her as a few years older, but why quibble? "I'd like you to meet Celia Miller. Celia, this is Doreen Abernathy and Heather Blythe." I'd explained the women's relationship earlier, as well as the undercurrents with Fred.

The sisters regarded each other uncertainly. I doubted any rule of etiquette covered this situation.

Danielle and Fred reached us. Their eyes widened, too, at

the full impact of Celia's resemblance.

The hush didn't last long. "I'm your sister, Danielle." A hand thrust out, grasping Celia's. Nearly the same height, the two could have been mirror images if not for their different attire.

"I'm Celia." My companion swallowed.

"This is my husband, Fred." While they shook hands, Danielle said, "I agree with the pastor. Each of us deserves forgiveness. When I got your letter, I was angry, but not any more. I'd like to get better acquainted."

When Doreen squirmed, Heather spoke up. "The resemblance is striking. If she's staying in the area, we can hardly ignore her, honey."

"True," Doreen conceded. "I suppose we should talk."

"Let's get out of this wind," Danielle said. "There's food and coffee inside, or hot chocolate if you prefer."

"I love hot chocolate." Celia smiled. "Especially with whipped cream and bittersweet sprinkles."

"Me, too," Danielle and Doreen said simultaneously.

Fred offered one arm to his wife and the other to her newfound sibling. "Great eulogy, wasn't it? We plan to attend his church tomorrow."

"I was impressed," Celia agreed. "Maybe I'll go, too, if it's okay."

"Of course," Danielle said.

"Billie suggested him." Doreen kept pace with them. "I liked his message."

I trailed behind with Heather. "Am I the only one who finds this situation weird?" she asked me.

"Everything about it is weird," I agreed.

Ahead of us, I spotted Tory blocking a photographer's attempt to push forward. Behind her, cameras clicked and reporters blathered to unseen viewers. Video of the three sisters would no doubt light up newscasts and go viral on the

Internet.

Indoors, a caterer had set up food and drinks in a private room. What I hadn't anticipated—nor had anyone—was that guests became confused on approaching the family. Some shook Celia's hand as if they'd met her before; a few called her Danielle or even, in a particularly uncomfortable moment, Dee Marie. She passed it off with a dip of the head and a soft thank-you-for-coming.

Danielle introduced her to Billie and Morris. Curiosity brought a tinge of color to Billie's cheeks, and she perked up as she spoke with Celia. She and Dee Marie had been close, I recalled.

Less than three weeks ago, Malerie had appeared in my office with her strange claim about a quadruplet. In retrospect, I believed she'd been confused by a combination of her dreams, grief and the unexpected sight of a ringer for Dee Marie. If only it had occurred to her sooner that this was the supposedly deceased child.

By the following day, she must have realized it. And in her hurry to confront Sandy, she'd unwittingly signed her own death warrant.

I emerged from my reflections to discover that the conversation had shifted. Learning that Celia worked in an obstetrical office, Danielle was sharing her and Fred's plans to hire a surrogate.

"We're not sure who'll be executor of Mom's estate—Heather's helping us sort that out—but with luck we'll inherit some money," she said. "It's terribly expensive, though. And then there's the egg donation business."

"You're lucky to have a sister who..." Celia halted. "I shouldn't assume anything."

Doreen stared at a group of guests across the room as if completely tuned out of this discussion. Heather took a swallow of coffee.

"As an egg donor?" Fred said. "We'll be looking elsewhere."

"Why not me?" Celia asked.

Doreen's jaw dropped. Heather choked on her coffee, but brought her coughing under control with admirable speed.

"That is, if it's acceptable to you," Celia added. "We are full sisters, genetically speaking. Isn't that right, Dr. Darcy?"

"True." Much as I respected her generosity, this wasn't a decision to reach lightly. "However, egg donation is complicated and carries certain risks." The drugs that stimulate egg production can have painful side effects, and the retrieval requires minor surgery.

"I do work in the field," Celia said dryly.

"Just being cautious." I left it at that. If she went forward with this, Safe Harbor's egg donor staff would ensure she was fully informed.

"It's a huge commitment," Danielle demurred.

"It would be an honor," Celia said. "You don't have to decide right away."

Other people approached, and the subject was dropped. Later, Celia declined my offer of a ride home. Fred and Danielle had invited her to dinner at their house.

I was glad to hear it. And for the chance to enjoy a little solitude.

The tall, dark-timbered house presented a longed-for refuge. When I entered from the garage, however, the expected rush of relief failed to materialize.

Ghostly memories swarmed. My fall down the stairs after learning of Lydia's death. The sight of the hand vacuum flying toward me and the water-filled tub. The horror as Sandy shoved Morris toward the railing. Damn. Would they ever fade?

In the front studio, late-afternoon light cast rainbows across the rack of clothing. I recognized a lacy white blouse and blue skirt Lydia had worn to a museum exhibit of the Dead Sea Scrolls. And remembered how a multicolored nightgown had sparked a night of lovemaking.

The pastor was right about moving past might-have-beens and should-have-dones. Sandy had let hatred eat her alive. I had to stop letting love eat *me* alive.

Time to reserve my favorite pieces and dispose of the rest. Install a safe for Lydia's jewelry when the police returned it. And accept that some questions could never be answered.

Through the bay window, I saw Lydia's car—Tory's car—pull into the driveway. When she spotted me, I hoped she'd join me, and she did.

"I have something to tell you." My sister-in-law seemed subdued in her dark suit, curly hair restrained by a ponytail band.

"Shoot." I lifted an empty cardboard box. "Okay if I start packing clothes for the thrift store while I listen? Tell me if there's anything you want."

"Lydia's clothes never fit me," she said.

Into the box I folded the blouse and skirt. "Dad used this room as an office. Maybe I'll do that." Sudden inspiration: "Or you could."

Tory shook her head. "Dad and I both feel we've been intruding. We're going to rent a place together."

Her statement shook me. Without realizing it, I'd counted on them staying. "If I've created that impression, I apologize. You're both welcome here."

"We've been underfoot long enough." No fishing; she meant it.

Two weeks ago, I'd searched for ways to keep her out. Why couldn't I be equally creative now? "Listen, Tory..."

"There's something else." The gravity in her tone halted my protest. "It's about Lydia."

216

"What about her?" I was only beginning to return to normal. Definitely not prepared for revelations.

Tory peered at a pair of dainty shoes jutting from a box, as if fascinated by the glitter. "According to the tour guide, my sister ate lunch with someone in Jerusalem."

"Who?" Could be a school friend who'd moved to Israel, I supposed, although Lydia had never mentioned anyone.

"She was secretive about it, according to Benjamin, the guide," she said. "He happened to hear her on the phone making arrangements."

"I wasn't aware she knew anyone in Israel. But what's the big deal?"

"When I tried to track the calls on her phone, the incoming and outgoing numbers didn't match, and none of them were in service," Tory said.

"That's strange."

"I thought so, too."

It reminded me of a spy movie, but the notion of my wife mixing in international skullduggery was preposterous. "What do you suppose it means?"

Tory shrugged. "I'm clueless, which is why I didn't bother you with it. It's possible she was connecting with a fellow artist or a gallery owner to discuss representation, or renting studio space."

Lydia had intended to live in Israel? *Don't jump to conclusions. She might have toyed with spending part of a year there.*

"Why share this now?" I asked.

"Keith told me about your bathtub incident." She cast me a hint of a smile. "What a chump. Anyway, I'd hate for you to die without hearing the whole story, such as it is."

"Your reaction to my near-death is that I'm an idiot?" I kept my tone light.

"If the shoe fits," she teased, and waved at the sparkly pair. "Speaking of shoes, you can chuck those. In fact, please do."

I seized on the opening. "In view of my gullibility, you should stay to provide extra security."

"Eric..."

"Don't leave," I said.

She regarded me questioningly.

I had to be frank. "You and Morris belong here. You're my family."

Tory's gaze swept my face. Seeking an answer? To what question?

Finally, she said, "You sure?"

"Unless you're moving in with Keith again."

She snorted. "Living with him was a mistake. We both like to be in control and we both have trust issues. We're friends, that's all."

To close the deal, I said, "I'll throw in Thanksgiving dinner. I'll cook it myself." Common sense raised its ugly head. "Or buy it."

"You host. We'll cook," Tory said. "Did you mean it about my using this room as an office?"

She was agreeing to stick around. Warmth spread through me. "Sure."

"Good. It's a tight squeeze at Fact Hunter. I'd rather work from here."

With a quick call to Morris, we settled our living arrangements. As for whatever Lydia's business had been in Jerusalem, perhaps someday the truth would emerge, but that day wasn't this day.

A few weeks later, we celebrated Thanksgiving. I learned later that Fred and Danielle set their table for six, including Billie and Celia. They all drank a toast to Heather and Doreen's engagement, although, I gathered, not necessarily with Fred's best wine.

In addition to dispensing her investment profits, Heather had offered to buy Rafe's practice and employ his staff. While it might be a practical business move, it also served as a goodwill gesture. I was sure Billie could use the money.

In my dining room, we were five, including Keith and my brother-in-law, Barry. At Morris's request, Tory lit candles, bowed her head and said a prayer in Hebrew.

In the timeless glow, for an instant, I saw Lydia's face. Until then, I hadn't noticed how strongly Tory's bone structure resembled her half-sister's.

No more ghosts were allowed at our table. Only gratitude that we had weathered a difficult year, and that cooks more gifted than me had prepared our food.

The End

ABOUT THE AUTHOR

USA Today bestselling author Jacqueline Diamond is known for her mysteries, romantic comedies, medical romances and Regency romances—more than a hundred titles. A former Associated Press reporter and TV columnist, Jackie has sold novels to a range of publishers including Harlequin, St. Martin's Press, William Morrow and Five Star Mysteries. Jackie and her husband, the parents of two grown sons, live in Southern California.

The Safe Harbor Medical mystery series includes *The Case of the Questionable Quadruplet, The Case of the Surly Surrogate, The Case of the Desperate Doctor* and *The Case of the Long-Lost Lover*. The mysteries share a setting and some secondary characters with her Safe Harbor Medical romance series.

More information about the author and her books is available on her website, www.jacquelinediamond.net.

If you enjoyed the book and would post a short review on your favorite on-line book site, it would help other readers discover it. Thank you!